THE WAY BACK

Hannah Rae

Thanks for reading!
—Hannah Rae

D1713846

KDP

ISBN 9798844487170

Visit the author online:
www.heyheyhannahrae.com
www.facebook.com/HeyHannahRae

For C.K.
He knows why.

And for N.B.,
because he posed a very poignant question
at exactly the right time.

"Days to decades, aware of 'em all,
And sometimes the words don't mean nothin' at all.
A noun, a verb, a sentence, a phrase.
There's no black and white; it's all fuckin' grey.
A stampede of storm clouds, swirling. Unclear.
A tangle of feelings that shouldn't be feared."

-Sebastian Porter,
"Running Through the Words"

JONNY.

Thursday, 3:18p.m. (EDT)

Until the words pop out of his mouth, Jonny Rockford isn't intending to mention anything about it to his friend, but the sentence escapes his lips of its own volition: "I've been toying with the idea of proposing to Alex."

Owen, who'd been about to take a bite of his burger, sets the sandwich on his plate and arches his eyebrows instead. "'Toying with the idea'?" he confirms.

Jonny nods and slides a hand into a pocket of his cargo shorts. The velvet covering of the tiny, hinged box is soft beneath his fingertips. Debating whether he should provide additional information, his hand, like his mouth, makes the decision for him. "I, uh... I bought a ring."

"Sounds like you've done a bit more than toy with the idea," Owen grunts, wiping his fingers on a napkin before gingerly picking up the box. Inside, a solitary diamond glimmers from its positioning on a slim band of silver. "Hold on, wait. You carry it around with you? How long've you had this?"

"Since March."

"*March?*"

The reaction is legitimate. It's now July and Jonny has yet to pop the question.

"Good lord, man! What're you waiting for?"

"I don't know?"

Jonny forms the answer as a question because the reality is... he *doesn't* know. He's thirty years old—a reasonable age to marry and start a family with the woman he's been seeing for the past four years—but for some reason, he's hesitant to take the next step. Tucked away in the back of his mind, he suspects he *might* have an idea as to why he's so reluctant to move forward with the proposal, but never in a million years does he plan to admit—

"It has something to do with that woman, doesn't it?"

"What woman?" Jonny wonders, attempting to play dumb, but Owen rolls his eyes and tosses a French fry at him, hitting Jonny square in the chest. "That *woman*," he repeats, emphasizing the second word. "The one you met in Denver all those years ago. I forget her name. Pippa? Poppy? It was something like that."

"Piper," Jonny whispers. He plucks the fry from his lap and tosses it to a seagull cackling overhead. Though it's a hot day, and humid, the seabreeze makes the outdoor dining experience just bearable. He reaches for his beer, the plastic cup perspiring excessively in the brilliant sunshine and creating a ring of moisture on the red-and-white plastic tablecloth. Flip's is known for its shrimp salad sandwiches and cheesy crab fries, but Jonny, like Owen, has opted for a cheeseburger. "Her name was Piper," he says a bit more loudly, and takes a long sip of his golden lager. "She was from Oregon."

After graduating from college and securing a teaching position at the local high school, Jonny Rockford had, on a whim, decided to travel out west by himself. He'd left Moonglow, North Carolina, early one Sunday morning in late July, driving away from the Atlantic and toward adventure. Single and only a few weeks shy of his twenty-fourth birthday, he'd ricocheted from one national park to the next, visiting Mammoth Cave and the Hot Springs, Carlsbad Caverns and the Petrified Forest. He'd made it the whole way to California before boomeranging back home, taking a more northern route this time and passing through Nevada, Utah, and Colorado.

It had been in Denver, at a hole-in-the-wall Mexican restaurant, that he'd met Piper for both the first and last time. She'd sidled up next to him at the bar and claimed the seat beside his, ordering a margarita with salt. Nearly black hair, incredibly green eyes, and lips that glistened beneath a fresh coat of colorless gloss. She'd been beautiful in a way that didn't require makeup, and as a result, she hadn't been wearing any. "What's good here?" she'd wondered, perusing a laminated menu.

"Not sure," Jonny answered in his slow, southern drawl. "This is my first time."

"What're you doing in Denver?"

"Just passing through. What about you?"

"Heading home. My flight was canceled. I booked another, but it won't leave 'til early tomorrow morning and I was super sick of the airport. Now I'm here." She'd shrugged and smiled... and that had been the beginning of a five-hour date of sorts.

"So what?" Owen asks now, drowning his fries in a combination of ketchup and mustard. "You bought the ring but you're not gonna use it

3

because of a woman you met six years ago and haven't talked to since? That's crazy, man. Alex is a sweet girl. She adores you. Are you afraid she's gonna say no or something?"

Quite the opposite, actually. What worries Jonny is that Alex will immediately agree to be his wife and then spend the next year planning the most elaborate wedding imaginable. Which is *fine*... but not necessarily what he wants, because as much as he loves his girlfriend, she often requires more maintenance than he would prefer.

"No, it's not that. I just... I wonder, you know?"

"You wonder what? If Alex is the right one?"

"I don't know. Maybe?"

Owen shakes his head, a look of disbelief washing across his chubby face. "I know you, Jonny. You're thinking about trying to track down the mysterious Piper, aren't you? What do you even know about her? She's from Oregon, okay. What else? Do you have a last name?"

"You know I don't."

"So what else can you tell me about her, huh? How do you intend to find her?"

"I don't know. She's a photographer."

"And?"

"And she's from a small city called Radio Park."

"And?"

"And her dad has a lot of tattoos."

Owen rolls his eyes.

"I know, I know. But I've gotta give it a shot, don't I? I can't *not* try to find her. 'Cos if I don't at least look, I'll always wonder, and *that* isn't a healthy start to a marriage."

"You do realize all these things you 'know' about her might be completely outdated, right? I mean, that was *years* ago, Jonny. She could've moved, or gotten a new career. And you're thinking... what? Put some gas in the car, pack a week's worth of clothes, and head west? That's crazy."

"Crazy" is an understatement; Jonny understands the odds of unearthing a needle in a haystack and is aware that's essentially what he'll be doing.

"I'm gonna fly," he says softly, taking another sip of his beer. He'd priced tickets earlier this morning.

"What about Alex? What're you gonna tell her?"

Not one to lie, this is the hardest part of his plan. "I have a buddy from college who lives in Bend. It's, like, a fifteen-minute drive from Radio Park. I'll tell her I'm staying with Artie. He's been begging me to visit for a couple years now, so this'll be a two-birds, one-stone sorta thing."

Jonny *will* make it a point to catch up with his old friend.

What he'll share with Alex is a mere half-truth rather than a full-fledged fabrication.

Looking skeptical, Owen narrows his eyes and chews the inside of his cheek. "I don't know, man. I'd be lying if I were to tell you I think it's a good idea because, well... I really don't. But I doubt my opinion matters much. You're gonna do what you want, aren't you?"

No longer hungry, Jonny covers the remainder of his burger with a paper napkin and pushes the plate away. An inch of beer sits in the bottom of his glass and he drains this in one gulp, dragging the back of his hand over his mouth before saying, "I *need* to do it. I don't know why, but I do. My goal is to fly out on Monday."

JANE.

Friday, 6:09p.m. (EDT)

Jane turns to face Marcus as he pulls his car alongside the curb of the terminal and turns on his four-ways. He's still wearing the work clothes he'd donned earlier this morning, his tie now loosened and his shirtsleeves rolled to reveal tanned forearms. His hair, curly and honey-colored, is mussed after a day of running his long fingers through it. Jane knows her boyfriend is a fan of math, but because she isn't, it's hard to imagine him feeling anything but sheer misery when he sets off to work at the accounting firm where he's employed. "It's really not so bad," he tells her all the time. "I actually *enjoy* crunching numbers."

Studying him now, she takes in his tired smile and the slight creases around his eyes. "I'll see you in a week," she says. "Your flight's supposed to land at two, isn't it?"

"Correct. And the rehearsal dinner is at what time? Six?"

"Yeah, but it's going to be pretty low-key. Crabs and beer in the Fergusons' backyard. No need to dress up." She turns in her seat, reaches back to touch the head of the wiry terrier sitting behind her. "And you'll drop Dennis at the kennel on Thursday night? He needs to be there by seven."

"I know, Janie. It's included in the three-page note you hung on the refrigerator." He rolls his eyes, but not in a way that suggests exasperation. "It's all going to run very smoothly. Are you sure you don't need help with your bags?"

She's managed to fit everything—Marcus's formal attire, her bridesmaid dress, and a week's worth of other clothes included—into one large suitcase and another small carry-on. "I can manage," she assures him.

The air, as she exits the car, is sticky and odorific. It reeks of diesel and cigarette smoke; July's heat makes it feel almost as if she's being wrapped in a stinky blanket. Having vacated the front seat, Dennis hops into it, placing his paws on her chest and initiating several licks to her chin. "I'll miss you too," she says, lifting him in order to offer a proper hug, "but I'll see you in ten days. I love you, Denny. Be a good boy for Marcus."

Fighting back tears, she returns him to the car and closes the door.

Marcus retrieves her luggage from the trunk and places it on the sidewalk, then opens his arms for a final hug. Jane can smell the minty, alpine scent of his deodorant as she buries her face against his chest. Tall and rather gangly, his arms feel surprisingly strong as he wraps them around her and holds her tight. "I'll see you on Friday," he whispers. "It'll be here before you know it."

"You're probably right."

"Call when you get to Piper's, okay? No matter how late it is."

"I will."

"And Janie?"

"Hmm?"

He kisses her forehead, then pulls away so he can meet her gaze when he says, "Have fun."

10:38p.m. (PDT)

A forty-five-minute layover in Seattle allows Jane exactly enough time to secure a venti cappuccino from Starbucks before making her way to the appropriate gate. When she boards her flight, still nursing the heavily caffeinated beverage, the woman in the neighboring seat eyes the large cup and exclaims, "Oof! You must have a long way to go if you're drinking *that* right before midnight!"

Jane laughs. "Actually? No. Redmond's my last stop, but my cousin's picking me up at the airport and we haven't seen each other for almost two years. I'm preparing for a long night."

"To be young and have that sort of stamina again! Ha!"

The woman doesn't appear to be old by any means—no more than forty, surely—but Jane supposes the idea of *beginning* a night of drinking at midnight or later does sound like something a college student might do. "I'm twenty-eight," she admits, stifling a yawn. "Believe me: a start time of tomorrow morning is *not* how I usually operate. This is a special occasion. Piper's getting married next weekend."

"A wedding! That's fun. Do they live in Redmond?"

"Radio Park. It's about a twenty-minute drive from Redmond."

"I know Radio Park quite well. My sister lives there. Beverly. She and my other sister, Esther, and I make it a point to meet for a week each summer and spend some time together. We were always close growing up, but now we're scattered across the country. Esther lives in Tucson and I'm in the Chicago area."

"Esther, Beverly, and... what's *your* name?"

"Muriel. Our mother loved traditional, older-sounding names." She shrugs. "What about you?"

"Jane. It sounds like my mother and your mother have similar tastes!"

"It really does, doesn't it?" Muriel smiles and fiddles with the safety belt around her waist. Both women listen attentively as the flight attendant runs through which exits to use in case of an emergency and how to position oxygen masks, but as the plane starts down the runway, they resume their previous conversation. Muriel asks about the wedding and wonders how Jane feels about her cousin's fiance.

"In all honesty," she responds, "I'm not sure. I have yet to meet him. The two started dating about a year ago and things have moved really quickly. I don't know why Piper's in such a rush to get married, but she is." Jane lifts her shoulders in a display of puzzlement; she really *has* wondered about the urgency fueling this particular wedding. The couple got engaged only seven months after getting together. "When you know, you know," Piper had said over the phone when she called to break the news, but Jane isn't sure she completely agrees with this sentiment. She and Marcus have been together for more than three years and she's one-hundred-percent certain he *is* the one, but neither of them is in a big hurry to tie the knot.

"To each her own," she figures, but still feels the situation is a bit out of character for her cousin. Unlike other women her age, Piper has never taken an interest in fashion or makeup; nine times out of ten, her hair is unstyled and her clothes are ill-fitting. Slim and muscular, she looks good in just about anything, but it's rare she wears something that shows off her figure. One of the many things that strikes Jane as odd about the upcoming wedding, however, is the amount of detail being paid to dresses, fingernails, and updos. She's never known Piper to wear nail polish, but for some unknown reason, it's become imperative that every bridesmaid receive both a manicure *and* a pedicure.

Jane passes a good chunk of the ninety-minute flight by conversing with Muriel. They talk a bit about the wedding and a lot about the interesting restaurants Radio Park has to offer. "You absolutely *must* visit The Library," Muriel instructs. "It's a bar that's actually *inside* an old library! I was there three years ago and can't wait to go back! All of the drinks are named after books and authors."

As an English major, this is right up Jane's alley. She makes a mental note to go there with Piper.

By the time the pilot comes over the loudspeaker and announces they'll be landing in just a few moments, Jane's cappuccino has kicked in and she's feeling excited to reconnect with her cousin. She fastens her safety belt once more, puts her seat in its most upright position, and prepares to return to earth.

Saturday, 1:57a.m. (PDT)

"What time do the bars close out here?"

Jane asks the question as she swirls the last few sips of her gin and tonic. The melting ice cubes clink against the side of her glass, faintly audible in the quiet night. Piper has brought her to an unusual spot known as the Watering Hole. Western in nature, the interior is adorned with horseshoes and vintage wanted signs, the bartenders wear cowboy hats and bandanas, and the music being piped into the dimly lit interior consists primarily of Hank Williams, Loretta Lynn, and Johnny Cash. Outside, however, a few decorative hay bales and wagon wheels are the only things that hint at the establishment's theme.

"Most places close at two, but this one's open 'til three. If you want another drink, there's time."

"I shouldn't. I'm exhausted, Pipe. I've been awake for, like, almost twenty-four hours straight. I forgot how much of an impact the three-hour time difference has on me when I fly out here." She yawns into the crook of her elbow, trying to summon another thirty minutes' worth of energy.

Piper nods in a show of understanding. "Alright. Let's finish our drinks and head home. I thought you could crash with me tonight. Tomorrow, at a more reasonable hour, I'll drive you over to my parents' house. There's a lot more space and you'll be able to have your own room. Does that sound okay?"

Though she hasn't stayed there for years, Unc and Aunt Sophie's house is one of her favorite places to visit. A sprawling farmhouse on the outskirts of Radio Park, the home's eclectic decorative style is incredibly unique. Each member of the Ferguson family has his or her own artistic ability and one of Sophie's fortes is interior design; the patterned walls, vibrant colors, and interesting art can be overwhelming at times, but the home is ultimately a delight for one's eyes.

"I'd love that," Jane assures her. "When will I get to meet Max?"

Piper's eyes twinkle at the mention of her fiancé's name. Uncharacteristically, she's applied a shimmery coat of shadow and some mascara that makes her lashes appear even longer than they are. The makeup's effect is irises that gleam every bit as green as freshly mown grass. "Sunday night," comes her response, the word paired with a subtle giggle. "He wants to take us to dinner."

"Sunday night," Jane repeats through yet another yawn. "I look forward to it."

JONNY.

Saturday, 6:07a.m. (EDT)

Unable to sleep, Jonny abandons the idea of slumber and throws back the covers, placing his feet on the floor. Beside him, Alex stirs. She'd stayed over last night, just as she does most weekends; the two had grilled shrimp kabobs, split a bottle of wine, and watched a silly romantic-comedy with an unbelievable happily-ever-after ending. Already, he's forgotten the gist of the plot.

"Where are you going?" Alex asks, her eyes squinting open. "It's early."

"To the beach. I'll be back in an hour or two. Want me to grab coffee on my way home?"

She smiles and reaches up to place her hand on his neck, pulling him down for a kiss. "Please," she whispers as her lips brush against his. "Get me something sweet."

Slipping from the room, Jonny pads through the house naked, pulling on a pair of diving shorts and then wiggling into his wetsuit. He allows the Short John to hang open for now, excess neoprene bunching around his waist. Outside, the sound of the ocean pounding the shore is audible from two blocks away. The air smells briny and seagulls cackle overhead, swooping through the blue-grey light of the morning. Jonny grabs his board from the porch and slides his feet into a worn pair of sandals, taking the narrow trail that will lead him to the beach. Gravel to pebbles to sand. The sun is fully awake by the time he mounds the dune and weaves his way around clumps of marram grass, eager to reach the water.

The waves are respectable today. They reflect the sun in ribbons of yellows and oranges. A mile or two from shore, a sailboat bobs its way along the coast, its sail a triangular wedge of rainbow. Jonny considers the other surfers. There are five of them: two on the shore and three in the water. Way out in the ocean, paddling parallel to the beach, he thinks he recognizes his student Chloe. That means one of the men in the water is likely her father. He knows the two regularly start their weekends with a search for the perfect wave.

It's been a week or two since Jonny last joined the early-morning crew. Now, as the waves lap at his ankles and the faint taste of salt coats his lips, he thinks this had been a mistake. Surfing, more than anything else, allows him the opportunity to organize his thoughts and clear his head, and as he paddles deeper into the ocean, the spray of cresting waves splashing against his face, he realizes that clearing his head is precisely what needs to be done. "Alex is a fantastic person," he tells himself, "and embarking on a search to locate Piper-from-Radio-Park is insane. What am I doing?"

"Putting to bed a curiosity that could haunt me for the rest of my life," he rationalizes. "If I don't do it now, I'll always wonder. It's worth a shot, isn't it?"

"It is," he decides as the ocean swells beneath him. He glances over his shoulder, positioning himself so as to catch the incoming wave. His body acts on its own, paddling and then rising lithely onto the board. "It's worth it," he mutters aloud. "It has to be worth it."

ANSEL.

The kitchen carries an odd aroma of coffee and turpentine. Suspecting the reason, Ansel's gaze first darts to the coffeemaker on the counter, noting the partially full pot, and then to the mason jar on the windowsill with the heads of three paintbrushes submerged in a few inches of muddy-colored liquid. Sophie, undoubtedly, had lost interest in cleaning her supplies and abandoned them for the time being.

Ansel retrieves a mug and fills it with the caffeinated brew, taking a long sip before rummaging in the cupboard for cereal. He dumps some granola into a bowl, tops it with a splash of milk and a handful of homegrown blackberries, and dines at the kitchen sink. As he eats, his eyes scan the front page of the newspaper, which his wife has propped against the drying rack. "This looks fun!" she's written in ballpoint pen. "Future breakfast date?"

Circled in blue ink, the below-the-fold story is all about Radio Park's newest coffeehouse: Cup o' Mud Buzz. Operated by two California natives, Ansel finds it interesting that the shop's sister store is actually located in Pennsylvania. Lara Abbott, one of the owners, is quoted as promising "a nitro cold brew that'll pack a punch, along with several delicious pastries from which to choose." The opening day, according to the article, is today.

"Whatcha readin'?"

Ansel glances up as his son wanders into the kitchen. Kai's hair is mussed from sleep, sticking up in the back and flattened on one side. He yawns as he stands in front of the open refrigerator, studying its contents.

"There's a new coffee shop in town, over on Bender Boulevard."

"Yeah? Just what Radio Park needs... more coffee." Kai chuckles and uncaps a container of orange juice. There's only an inch or two left in the bottle, but Sophie has trained her son well: he unearths a juice glass and uses that instead. "What time'll Janie be here?"

"Sometime this afternoon."

Kai rinses the plastic container and sets it in the sink to be recycled later. Then he snags a handful of blackberries and pops one into his mouth. "She'll stay in Piper's old room?"

"That's the plan."

"Is Max coming too?"

Though his son manages to voice the question without making a face, there's something in his tone that conveys a combination of hope and disgruntlement. Hope because he would prefer not to see his soon-to-be brother-in-law, disgruntlement because he realizes the odds of exchanging niceties with the man are high.

"I don't have that information," Ansel admits, "but I wasn't told he'd be in attendance."

Kai nods and exhales the smallest of sighs. "Good," he seems to say without saying, and rubs a hand through his disheveled hair. The question he *does* speak aloud is, "Where's Mom? In her studio?"

"I assume so. What're you getting into today?"

"Work. My shift starts at four."

Six years younger than his sister, Kai will be a senior in college next semester, and though web design is his focus, he's devoted the summer to pulling pints at the Terrible Terrier over on Bender. He'll be just a few doors down from Cup o' Mud Buzz, which may come in handy on nights like tonight when he's scheduled to close.

Ansel rinses his bowl, loads the dishwasher, and refills his coffee. "I'm heading to the barn for a bit. That's where I'll be if you need me." He slips out the back door and cuts across the dusty yard. Grass grows in patches, but the ground consists largely of sandy soil. Receiving less than twelve inches of rain per year, Radio Park isn't known for its lush greenery. With this, however, comes the perk of not being known for its humidity either. The air this morning is dry and hot, the sun bright and gleaming overhead.

There'd been a time when the Fergusons operated a small storefront in the center of town. As their enterprise had grown and customers expressed an interest in viewing the couple's studio, there'd no longer been a need to manage two locations. Nowadays, they run their business out of the barn, with a vast display room at the front of the building and two studios at the back: one designated for Sophie's landscapes, the other reserved for Ansel's beautiful frames. Piper, having recently secured full-time employment with an up-and-coming event planning operation, still hangs a few of her photographs in her parents' shop. It's a black-and-white image of the desert that Ansel's eyes land on now as he enters the barn. The focus is a cactus, growing from a wedge of soil existing between two massive rocks, the juxtaposition of Radio Park's winding river coursing in the background far, far below.

"Sophie?" He needs to shout to be heard over the radio. The song isn't one he recognizes—he prefers classic rock rather than some of these newer trends—but his wife tends to enjoy much of what's popular today. Her voice, strong and slightly off-key, can be heard carrying from the back of the barn. "Sophie!" Ansel calls again, entering her work area and standing to the left of her easel.

Dressed in an old pair of overalls and a simple white tank top, his wife smiles up at him and continues singing, "*Fast is fast and slow is slow; / You need both speeds to make life go. / Reprieves are nice, but so's gusto: / A minute down, then uptempo!*" There's a smudge of blue on her chin and her dark hair is flecked with white. Some of this is paint and some is just a result of aging. She wears her straight locks piled atop her head and held in place by an angled paintbrush and a chewed pencil. "I love this song," she says. "It's so catchy!"

"I'm not familiar with it."

"Of course you aren't! I forget the band, but I love them. The lead singer's voice is just... Ah! I'll bet he's *very* sexy."

Ansel laughs and moves to stand behind Sophie, resting a hand lightly on her shoulder. "I'll bet he's very young." His eyes roam over the landscape she's working on, taking in the whimsical design: a meadow of poppies spread at the base of the Cascade Mountains. Nowhere in Radio Park does a field such as this one exist, but the image is both beautiful and captivating. "Looks like you're pretty close to done."

"I'm not happy with the sky quite yet, but it's getting there." She leans her head against her husband's belly and stares up at him. "Is Kai still sleeping?"

"Nope, he's up."

"I asked him to clean his bathroom before Janie gets here. Do you know if he did it?"

Knowing his son, Ansel can't imagine that Kai jumped right out of bed and set about performing this task before filling his stomach with breakfast. Not wanting to throw the young man under the bus, however, he responds with, "He didn't mention it, but that doesn't mean it hasn't been done. I was planning on framing a few pieces for Rufus Longfellow this morning. If you need me to finish up anything in preparation for Jane's arrival, though, I'm happy to—"

"Nope, you do what you need to do. With the exception of that bathroom, everything's ready."

Ansel bends down to kiss her forehead, then heads next door to busy himself with his project.

JONNY.

Saturday, 10:18a.m. (EDT)

"It'll only be for a week," Jonny says as he scrolls through his flight options. "Artie's been asking me to visit for years. I've got the time, so I'm gonna do it. You're working nights next week anyhow; it's not like we'd see much of each other."

His girlfriend sighs heavily. It's obvious she'd prefer he not go, but his statement *is* accurate. Alex works as a veterinary technician at a twenty-four/seven emergency clinic and is required to complete third-shift hours one week out of every month. For that time period, she sleeps when it's light and works when it's dark and Jonny is left to his own devices.

This month, he'll merely be left to his own devices in a different state.

Alex comes up behind him and studies the computer screen over his shoulder. Her fingers tickle the back of his neck, move north to softly pet his buzzed scalp. "Who's Artie again? Have I ever met him?"

"Once, at Bruiser's wedding. Arturo Beltran. We were roommates freshman year."

"Oh."

Jonny wouldn't expect her to remember him. The men certainly don't speak on a regular basis; the last time they were together was three years ago, when another college pal—Bruce Marconi—married his long-time girlfriend at a resort on Sanibel Island. It had been a beautiful wedding, and the first time he and Alex had left the state together. They'd turned the long weekend into a week and enjoyed a relaxing vacation, returning to Moonglow well-rested and a bit sunburnt.

Pushing the memory from his mind, Jonny clicks on a flight with three layovers: one in Charlotte, another in Chicago, and finally a third in Phoenix. He'd prefer a more direct route, but the reasonable price is worth making a concession. Before he can change his mind, he books the flight and fumbles for his credit card, using the two-finger method to plug in the numbers. Ignoring his girlfriend's distracting touch, he once more scans the specifics and confirms the purchase. "Done," he sighs, leaning back in his chair. "I'll fly out early on Monday and get back on Sunday."

"Mmm-hmm."

Jonny thinks he detects the hint of a pout in Alex's tone, but it's hard to be sure, so rather than comment on it, he reaches for his lukewarm coffee and takes a long swallow. Though his thoughts probably ought to be focused on the buxom blonde trying desperately to capture his attention, it's the word "Piper" that continues to flit through his brain.

JANE.

Saturday, 2:58p.m. (PDT)

Unlike other barns, the exterior of the Fergusons' studio and workshop is a myriad of colors. Years and years ago, each horizontal slat had been painted a different shade: red, orange, yellow, green, blue, indigo, violet. The result? A now-weathered, beautifully undulating rainbow that exudes cheerfulness. Jane finds herself smiling as the structure comes into view.

"You've always loved that barn," Piper laughs, noting her cousin's goofy grin.

"Because it's *so different* from anything I grew up with! I love my parents, but they were born without whimsy bones... I still sometimes think about how you once said your dad might've been adopted. He really is completely different from that side of the family!"

"He's excited to see you. They all are."

She guides her hatchback past the barn and into the driveway, parking behind her father's truck. Even before the ignition has been shut off, Sophie is exiting the house and hurrying toward them. As her niece climbs from the car, she wraps her in a warm embrace. She smells of lemon and turpentine. "Look at you!" she exclaims, pulling away in order to properly study the young woman. "Your curls are just... *perfect!*"

"Yeah, well. This no-humidity climate does wonders for my hair," Jane laughs, running a hand over her strawberry tresses. She considers her aunt's paint-splattered overalls and the smudges of green on her hands. "You appear to've been having an artistic day!"

"Always," Sophie assures her. She wraps an arm around Jane's waist and guides her up the steps to the front porch. "Leave the luggage, Piper. We'll send Kai out to get it."

From the outside, the farmhouse looks much like other farmhouses: its siding is white, its gables are peaked, and its porch is sprawling. Wicker ceiling fans, mounted on either side of the front door, lazily circulate the dry Oregon air; a wooden bench and four rocking chairs, no doubt built by Ansel, provide ample seating. Jane hopes that at some point during her visit she's able to sit out here with her uncle, reminiscing about the past and pondering what the future may bring. With any luck, these deep conversations will occur while nursing a glass of Ansel's famous blackberry tea. Just thinking about the cool, sweet beverage causes her tastebuds to tingle, and perhaps it's because her thoughts are elsewhere that she's taken a bit off guard when entering the home. Although Jane is fully aware of what to expect, the busily patterned walls, vibrantly colored furniture, and intricately patterned rug make for a jarring experience. It's as if her eyes don't know where to look first!

"Uh-oh." A deep chuckle escapes Ansel as he joins the women in the foyer. "You've done it again, Sophie: the poor girl's completely overstimulated!" His big arms enfold Jane, executing the tightest of hugs. "How are you, Janie-girl? It's been too long."

"It has," she agrees. "I've missed you, Unc."

She hadn't expected to cry, but as Jane inhales his familiar scent of wood chips and chicory, she realizes her cheeks are damp. Releasing her uncle, she wipes at the tears and smiles through them, taking in the tall man before her.

For those unfamiliar with Ansel Ferguson, his appearance might evoke an aura of unease or intimidation. He's a big fellow, with a wide stature and a height of six-foot-five. His head is shaved, his dark beard is unruly, and his eyes are every bit as green as his daughter's. When Ansel smiles, his entire face lights up, and it's then that people are able to look past his many tattoos to see the genuinely kind spirit of the man.

Ansel had begun acquiring ink at a fairly young age. His first addition had been an anchor on the inside of his left bicep. Since then, the artwork has evolved into a nautical sleeve that encases his arm, wraps around his back and chest, and wanders halfway down his right forelimb. The skin from his hand to his elbow is a clean slate but for the compass tattooed on his wrist. No larger than a fifty-cent piece, the image is deep blue and intricately detailed. This is Jane's favorite. As a child, she'd often traced its shape, feeling her uncle's pulse beneath her fingertips as he and her father chatted about life and family, their quiet voices rumbly in their chests.

Placing a large hand on Jane's shoulder, Ansel clears his throat and says, "You look great, kid. Are you thirsty? I made a fresh batch of blackberry tea just for you."

"How could I possibly say no to that?"

She follows her uncle into the kitchen and is momentarily startled to find a lanky young man leaning against the counter. He wears loose khakis, black Converse sneakers, and a brown t-shirt printed with the silhouette of a large dog. "Hey, cuz."

Kai appears to have grown at least three inches since the last time Jane saw him. Always reminiscent of a character in a Ray Bradbury novel or one of the many youths depicted in Norman Rockwell's paintings, he will likely retain a perpetual boyishness regardless of his height. Still, she can't believe how much older he appears. "How are you the same kid I used to chase fireflies with?"

A novelty for her west-coast cousins, it had been a tradition to fill several mason jars with the glowing beetles each time the Fergusons traveled east during the summer months.

With cheeks turning rosy, Kai rolls his eyes and walks over to give Jane a hug. "For the record, the bathroom's remarkably clean right now. I even scrubbed the tub."

"I'm flattered you went to so much trouble!"

Sophie gives her son a playful swat as she crosses the kitchen to retrieve a few glasses and fill them with ice cubes. "None for me, Mom," Kai says. "I've gotta be at work pretty soon." Then, catching Jane's eye, he points to his shirt and says, "I tend bar at the Terrible Terrier. It's a brewery in town."

"You can't be old enough to serve alcohol!"

"What?" he laughs. "Yeah! I turned twenty-one, like, six months ago!"

"Oh my *gosh*. You're becoming a full-fledged man!"

Blushing more deeply, he shrugs and acknowledges, "Yeah, I guess so."

"Kai," Sophie says, "will you bring in Jane's luggage before you leave? And carry it up to the guest room?"

"It's really my old room," Piper whispers, "but they've changed things around since I flew the coop. The good news is, the walls aren't flamingo pink anymore. The bad news, though? You'll have to share a bathroom with Pigsty Kai."

"Oh, that shouldn't be too terrible," Jane whispers back. "I heard he cleaned it before I got here." She gives her younger cousin a wink as he walks away to retrieve her bags. Then, accepting a glass of tea from her aunt, she says more loudly, "It's so good to see you guys. I can't believe it's been two years since we were in the same place at the same time! Fill me in on what's new. Have you done anything more to the house? What sorts of art projects are you working on these days? Tell me everything! Please! We no doubt have a lot to catch up on..."

8:33p.m. (PDT)

The temperature has dropped considerably and the windows to the sprawling farmhouse are now open. Inside, the getting-ready-for-bed sounds of Sophie can be heard: the whistle of a teakettle, the creak of old floorboards settling, the grumble-rumble of pipes as a hot bath is run. Piper left half an hour ago and Kai won't be home until the wee hours of morning, but Jane is more than content to pass the time with her uncle.

As Ansel rocks, the melodic tinkle of ice cubes can be heard clinking around in his sweating glass of blackberry tea. It's been a long time since he's partaken in alcohol—twenty years, at least—but Jane knows he still attends meetings from time to time. She'd been surprised when her aunt pulled a bottle of wine from the refrigerator earlier today; only rarely do the Fergusons have booze in the house. At least, that had been the case when she stayed with them two years ago. She supposes it's possible times have changed, especially with Kai tending bar at one of the local breweries, and as she takes a small sip of the white zinfandel her aunt had instructed her to finish, she asks tentatively, "Are you sure it doesn't bother you that I'm drinking this, Unc?"

"Not at all," Ansel assures her. "I won't say I never struggle with cravings, but today hasn't been much of a challenge. It's good to have you back with us, Janie-girl. How's that boyfriend of yours? I gather things are going well since you're still together..."

"Marcus is great. We moved to Philly at the end of last year and have a small apartment together. It's only a ten-minute commute for him and, I mean, I'm able to work from home most days." Although her role as copy editor isn't always enjoyable, this particular aspect of the job is definitely a perk. "Did I tell you I got a puppy? Dennis. He's not really a puppy anymore—he's almost a year old—but that hasn't affected his energy level."

"Some sort of terrier, right? I think Piper mentioned it."

"A wire-haired fox terrier, yes! He's absolutely adorable."

"And you named him Dennis, huh?"

Jane laughs. "Partly because he's a menace, but also because I think it's a funny name for a dog." She sets her wine glass on the porch railing and pulls her feet onto the rocking chair, wrapping her arms around her knees.

"It sounds as though I'll finally be introduced to Max tomorrow evening. Pipe says he's taking us to dinner."

"Oh, yeah?" Though there's nothing in Ansel's words to suggest distaste, his mild tone definitely conveys a hint of impassivity. "Where're you going? Do you know?"

"I didn't ask." She furrows her brow as she studies her uncle. "You're not a fan of Max?"

"I didn't say that."

"Your face implied it."

In the soft glow of the light filtering through drawn curtains, Ansel's mouth quirks into a wry grin. "He's just... very different from what I imagined for my daughter," he says slowly, searching for the right words. His voice, deep and gritty, is barely audible in the quiet night. The mellifluous hoot of an owl sounds from somewhere in the distance as Ansel clears his throat. "He's quite a few years older than she is, and not at all artistic... but she loves him."

Jane reaches for her wine, holding the stemmed glass but not taking a sip.

Her uncle drains the last of his iced tea. "I'll be curious to learn what you think of him," he admits, lifting himself to his feet. "Max is an intelligent guy. Very charming."

"His family has quite a bit of money, don't they?"

"Oh, yeah."

"And he's a lawyer?"

"A defense attorney," Ansel confirms. "Maxwell Terrence Storm, III, Esquire. It's a mouthful, isn't it?" The floorboards creak under his weight as he walks toward the door. "I'm gonna get a refill, Janie-girl. Do you need anything?"

"No thanks." Jane shivers and pulls the left sleeve of her sweatshirt over her hand. As the front door swings shut behind her uncle, she ponders Ansel's words regarding Max. "Not at all artistic." Just because Piper comes from a creative household and feels passionately about photography doesn't mean she needs to end up with someone who shares a similar background, but he *should* have an appreciation for her imagination. Even more so than before, she's eager to meet the mysterious fiance tomorrow... and wonders what her first impression will be.

JONNY.

Sunday, 1:15p.m. (EDT)

When Owen unexpectedly appears that afternoon with a six-pack, he's looking a bit disheveled. "What's up?" Jonny asks, taking in his rumpled shirt and mussed hair. "Everything okay?"

"Is Alex here?"

The question is a puzzling one. "No. She works tonight and ran home to spend some time with her cats before her shift. Why?"

Owen ignores this inquiry and pushes past his friend, trudging down the hall to the kitchen and setting the beer in the refrigerator. He twists off the cap of one bottle and takes a long sip, then glances at Jonny and arches his brows, wondering if he'd like a lager as well.

A nod indicates that he would.

"I'm packing," he says as he accepts the bottle. "If you wanna hang out, we're gonna have to do it in my bedroom."

The mattress is occupied by an open suitcase and several stacks of clothing: shirts, shorts, two hoodies, some jeans, and several pairs of clean-but-unfolded boxer briefs. Owen moves a basket of laundry from the chair in the corner and perches on it, leaning forward to rest his elbows on his knees. His belly spills into his lap. The man drinks far too many six-packs to actually *have* a six-pack, and it seems that with each passing year, he grows a little bit wider. Friends since middle school, Jonny has continued to watch this phenomenon occur. There'd been a time when he'd attempted to alter Owen's unhealthy habits, encouraging him to opt for a salad instead of a burger, or go for a walk instead of crashing on the couch and flipping through the channels. Having impacted his behavior not at all, Jonny's since abandoned the efforts and resigned himself to the fact that his best pal is a bit of a slob. Still, Owen appears even more unkempt than usual. It seems evident that something is on his mind. "So what's up?" Jonny repeats. "Why're you here?"

The heavyset man runs a hand over his chubby cheeks. They're dusted with a scruff of golden whiskers that strongly resemble peachfuzz. He takes a deep breath and meets his friend's gaze. "I think you're making a mistake," he says bluntly. "I don't think you should go to Oregon."

"It's only for a week, Owen."

"Right, I know. It's not the length of the visit that concerns me, man. It's the visit itself."

"I already bought the ticket. Artie's expecting me."

"Okay, so... yeah. I get that."

Jonny retrieves his favorite sneakers from the closet and puts them in his bag, waiting for Owen to continue. When he does, what he says is, "So maybe you *should* go—maybe that's actually fine—but maybe you *shouldn't* go searching for Piper."

"That's the whole point of the trip."

"Right, I know," Owen says for the second time. "I just think that maybe it shouldn't be. The point of the trip, I mean. You love Alex, right? If you didn't, you wouldn't've thought about marrying her and taken the initiative to buy a ring. *That* speaks volumes, man. *That's* what you should be focused on. Not some mysterious woman you met, like, six years ago."

Jonny acknowledges what his friend is saying.

He actually recognizes some of the truth contained within the argument.

But he *can't* simply forget about Piper. Since purchasing the engagement ring meant for Alex, thoughts of the green-eyed girl from Oregon have only intensified. He thinks of her constantly, remembering snippets of conversation they'd had over the course of their one night together. Remembering more and more with each passing day.

As Piper had sipped her margarita with salt, she'd told him of a Mexican restaurant in her hometown. "It's called Olé," she'd explained, "and the owner—his name's Jorge—makes *the best* guacamole you've ever had in your life. I don't know what he does to it, but it's amazing. Smooth, flavorful... always insanely fresh. If you're ever in Radio Park, you should give it a try. And definitely get the sea bass tacos as your entree; you won't be disappointed."

He'd asked her about her family and learned that she came from a long line of artists. "My grandfather on my mom's side was a painter and my grandma was an incredible seamstress. Weirdly, my dad's side of the family is way more into the maths and sciences. I've sometimes wondered if he was adopted because he's just so *different* from the rest of them."

34

"What's he like?"

"Big and burly, covered in ink. He makes frames for a living—like, picture frames for other people's art—but he also does other things with wood. A good bit of the furniture in our house consists of originals; he made all of the bookcases, quite a few chairs, and the bed frames for both my brother's and my beds."

Recalling the story now, Jonny straightens up and narrows his eyes, pondering these newly surfaced details. "She has a brother," he mutters aloud, "and her grandma was a seamstress." The quiet contribution halts Owen in mid-sentence, though Jonny hadn't been listening to any of the words pouring out of his mouth. He might've been reciting a recipe for tuna salad, for all he knows; Jonny's thoughts had been in the past.

"A grandma who sews," Owen points out, "isn't much to go on. Neither is the fact that she has a brother. Lots of people have brothers. You have two of 'em."

"Yeah, I'm aware," Jonny says with a roll of his eyes, "but thanks for the reminder."

"I'm just saying—"

"I know what you're saying, Owen. You don't want me to go. You think it's a bad idea. You're afraid I'm gonna fuck things up with Alex, or get my heart broken, or... *something*. But Owen?" He tucks a few pairs of socks into his sneakers and waits for his friend to meet his gaze. "Owen, I *have* to do this. I can't explain why because I don't really understand it myself... but I *have* to go out there and *attempt* to track her down. It's crazy, I know, but it's something I've gotta do. Can you... can you at least *try* to wrap your head around that? Please?"

Taking a deep breath, Owen rests his perspiring bottle of beer on his knee and stares at the floor. The sigh exits his body through his nostrils, the sound an audible *whoosh* in the quiet room. "I can try," he assents. "But Jonny?"

"Yeah?"

"Just... be careful, okay?"

ANSEL.

The aroma of woodchips hangs heavy in the air and flecks of dust glint in the sunlight filtering through open windows. Although he has a few items that need to be framed, Ansel prefers to allot Sundays to a more creative outlet. Today his intent is to finish piecing together a second Adirondack chair and then stain it. The pair will be given to Piper and Max as a wedding present—a gift that will be useful (and hopefully appreciated) for years to come.

As Ansel assembles one of the armrests and screws it into place, something agitates the inside of his right wrist. It's not a painful botheration, but rather a subtle tickle, and as he sets his screwdriver aside, he turns his attention to the compass tattooed there on his skin. Lately, the ink's been more active than usual. Ansel suspects this has something to do with his daughter's upcoming nuptials.

North is where the compass is meant to be pointing, but today its arrow tracks toward the east. "Illogical," he grumbles, running a calloused thumb over his skin, for he can never be certain just what it is the tattoo is attempting to convey. Almost imperceptibly, the needle waivers. It holds its position, however.

37

Ansel had been only seventeen when he'd acquired his first tattoo. Having grown up on the Maryland shore, his summers had always been spent on the water. Before he'd been legally old enough to hire, he'd assisted a fisherman by the name of Ol' Jeremiah. With a grizzled beard, sun-bleached eyes, and a grin shy of more than a few teeth, the elderly gentleman had been the spitting image of someone who might have worked alongside Captain Ahab. His boat was significantly smaller than the Pequod, though, and his interest was crabs rather than whales. Jeremiah paid his young employee under the table, which was acceptable through the boy's early teenage years.

At the age of sixteen, Ansel earned his lifeguard certification and spent the next summer on the beach. He made good money and his skin boasted a healthy tan all season long, but he missed being on the water. He'd rather have his feet on a boat than in the sand; he'd prefer to feel the rock of the ocean beneath him rather than lapping at his ankles.

He hung up his whistle the following year and went to work on a fishing rig slightly larger than Ol' Jeremiah's had been.

The boat was called the *Harvey John* and the crew was comprised of himself, a poetic twenty-something by the name of Cal Flannagan, and the vessel's captain, Susannah Lerner. Her hair was a mess of tangled curls that she often wore in a poorly constructed braid that hung down her back. Her forearms were covered in scars and ink, she'd lost the tip of her left index finger to a mangrove snapper while fishing off the coast of Florida in her early years, and when she laughed, the cackle that fountained up from deep in her belly was loud and abrasive. She referred to her employees always by their last names, and eventually shortened those to Flan and Ferg. It had been Susannah's lover—a married fellow who ran the local fish market and dabbled in art—who gave Ansel his first tattoo. Positioning it on the inside of his left bicep, the seventeen-year-old had managed to keep the blue-black anchor hidden from his parents for a good two months. They'd been disappointed to discover the ink, but the fallout had been minimal and shortly thereafter, Ansel began acquiring more and more art on his body: the wheel of a ship, two swallows on his chest, a message in a bottle, and a seductively clad mermaid. The designs, as a whole, are nautical... which is ironic since he now lives in a desert.

The compass was the last addition he'd made to his body, and it had been on a whim. Never in his wildest dreams had Ansel imagined he'd leave the eastern shore. He loved the briny scent of the ocean, the comforting soundtrack of rowdy gulls cackling above the deep-throated horns of tugboats approaching port. But he'd also never dreamed of falling in love.

The summer before her senior year of college, Sophie Sigmund traveled east to spend an entire month with her cousin Agnes in the little seaside town of Callensburg. The young women had been walking along the pier when Ansel came across them, having just finished a twelve-hour excursion on the *Harvey John*. He was sunburnt, sweaty, and reeking of fish. What he needed was a shower.

What he wanted was a beer.

"Grab a drink with me?" he'd said to Cal, and his studious sidekick had agreed.

Not wanting to turn the stomachs of diners visiting the local eateries, they'd purchased two six-packs of Budweiser and carried them down to drink on the docks. The men did this sometimes. Cal generally waxed poetic about the dying day and Ansel listened, occasionally asking a question about his pal's choice of description. "Look how the sun kisses the water with her painted lips," Cal might say. To which Ansel would wonder, "Do you always think of the sun as female?"

It seems likely that a conversation much like this one would have been had if Sophie and her cousin hadn't noticed the men and asked them where they'd gotten the beer. "We're only twenty," Agnes had admitted, "but we have money. We just... can't use it to *legally* buy alcohol."

Ansel had never intended to drink all six of his beers. It therefore seemed fitting to say, "We've got plenty. You can share with us if you'd like."

The women had exchanged a quick look, a single silent question passing between them, and then Sophie smiled up at the dark, burly man and said, "Sure!"

They'd kicked off their shoes and sat at the end of an empty dock, swinging their legs above the gentle waves. In addition to the noisy seagulls and echoes of faraway conversations, the evening boasted the subtle creak of ropes as they stretched to hold their charges. Buoys bobbed in the bay and the sun's "kiss" eventually faded to a mere memory. To this day, Ansel still recalls the way the warm, weathered wood of the pier felt against the backs of his legs. He remembers too how Sophie's leg felt pressed against his, and how she'd smelled faintly of sunscreen and bubblegum.

He hadn't kissed her that night, but he had gotten her number, and the two had squeezed in quite a few dates over the course of that month.

They'd kept in touch the following year, writing letters and talking on the phone and even visiting periodically, despite the distance. Originally from Oregon, Sophie attended school in Pittsburgh, so even though the two weren't especially close, they were closer than they could have been. And then, once she'd graduated, they began to talk about a future together.

"I love Oregon," Sophie had told him. "I'll leave if I have to, but it's not what I'd prefer."

She was the one with the college degree. Ansel's education had ended with the completion of his twelfth-grade year. He loved boats, but he loved Sophie more, and he knew that if he had to choose between the two, the latter is the one he would opt for. And so he'd packed all of his belongings into his pickup, hugged his family goodbye, and set off across the country.

But before leaving Callensburg, he'd made one final stop. At the local tattoo parlor that had done much of his work, he'd requested an impromptu appointment to have a compass added to the inside of his right wrist. "To remember the sea," he'd explained, "and to remind me of where I came from and where I'm going." He hadn't expected the compass to actually *move*. To this day, he doesn't understand how such a phenomenon even exists. But the compass isn't stagnant, and over the years, it's proven to be a useful tool in guiding him through difficult decisions.

Placing his left thumb atop the blue ink, he wonders just what it is that's trying to be shared now.

JANE.

Sunday, 5:43p.m. (PDT)

"Where are we going for dinner? Do I need to wear something dressier than a denim skirt, or will that suffice?" Jane straightens up and presses her cell phone closer to her ear. She'd spent the afternoon with her aunt, exploring some of Radio Park's small shops and visiting one of the many coffee shacks that are so prevalent in the Oregon town. Sophie had tried to convince her to get her caffeine fix from the newly opened Cup o' Mud Buzz, but Jane had refused. "I'm willing to check it out later in the week," she'd said, "but my first latte needs to come from one of the shacks, Aunt Sophie! Those coffee shacks are, like, one of my very favorite things about Radio Park!"

Just as Pennsylvania boasts parking-lot huts specializing in snow cones, Oregon does the same with cappuccino, macchiato, and espresso. Jane had splurged and gotten a frozen mocha sweetened with a shot of caramel. The barista had piled extra whipped cream on top, drizzled the decadent concoction with chocolate, and snapped a domed plastic lid onto the cup. "Enjoy!" she'd commanded, and Jane certainly had.

Still a bit jittery from so much sugar and caffeine, Jane is eager to consume something of substance. She's hoping for a casual venue; when Piper announces that Max will be taking them to The Library, she giggles

42

and exclaims, "No way! That's the restaurant my flying companion recommended to me!"

"Your flying companion?" Piper confirms. There's a smile hidden in her tone.

"Muriel. That was her name. We sat together on the flight from Seattle to Redmond."

"Well, I figured you'd appreciate The Library since you were an English major. I mean, even though I'm not an avid reader like you are, the menu is pretty fun. You'll get a kick out of it at the very least, but the food's actually incredibly tasty. And a denim skirt is fine; it's a casual place. I'll be at my parents' house by six-thirty, okay? Max got us a seven o'clock reservation."

"Yep! All that sounds great. I'll see you soon, Pipe."

7:03p.m. (PDT)

The Library is a two-story structure located a couple of blocks from the center of town. It sits higher than the other buildings, suggesting an air of importance; a sweeping set of marble stairs leads up to the front door, which is located in the middle of four massive pillars. The facade shines in the darkening night, its white bricks glinting in the streetlamps that line the road. "Are you *sure* I'm not underdressed?" Jane confirms. "This place looks intimidating!"

"I swear to you it's not," Piper assures her, though she's donned a little black dress. The fabric is cotton and the style is simplistic: spaghetti straps with an empire waist. She carries a red leather clutch in her left hand, a denim jacket draped over her arm. Her sandals are a step up from the rubber thongs Jane wears on her own feet, the soles *thwapping* against the steps as she keeps pace with her cousin.

Piper's stride is long and her speed is quick. They'd had trouble finding parking and are running a few minutes late. "Max is a stickler for being on time," she offers as explanation. "Tardiness is his biggest pet peeve."

"Oh." Although the information is vaguely interesting, Jane doesn't have much of a chance to process it. Her attention is immediately captured by the restaurant's interior as she follows Piper through the revolving glass door. Book covers—both modern titles and the classics—have been enlarged and framed. They hang on the dusky-hued walls, advertising the adventures of Tom Sawyer and Jo March, Ender Wiggin and Bridget Jones.

The entire back wall is comprised of floor-to-ceiling bookcases, the spines of the hardbacks and paperbacks arranged by color rather than alphabet. Like the Fergusons' barn, the effect is a rainbow: red to orange to yellow to green to blue to indigo to violet.

The bar itself is a rich mahogany that's well worn in places and glossy in others. Bottles of golden bourbon, dark rum, and crystal-clear vodka line the shelves, glistening in the glow cast by pendant lights. Reminiscent of the lamps often spotted on the desks of librarians and bankers, their domed shades are made of thick glass the color of clover.

Even the smell of The Library is somehow fitting, like cognac and sweet tobacco and that musty, familiar aroma that wafts up whenever a beloved novel is cracked open. Jane fills her lungs with the scent and holds it there for a moment, allowing her eyes to adjust to the dim lighting as they continue to scan the room. It's as they land on a narrow booth only a few yards away that she realizes the attractive man occupying it must be Piper's fiancé. He smiles in a way that could either be perceived as confident or smug—Jane isn't sure which. She smiles too, though, and follows her cousin over to the table.

Max has skin the color of coffee that's been doctored with a hearty splash of cream. His face is clean shaven and accentuated by high cheekbones and an angular jaw; his eyes, dark and alluring, twinkle as they land first on Piper, then on the woman beside her. As he gets to his feet, Jane is surprised to find that he's actually a bit shorter than she is... and therefore a bit shorter than his fiancé as well. "You must be Maxwell Terrence Storm, III, Esquire," she says. "It's nice to finally meet you."

"Call me Max," he chuckles, extending a hand and greeting her with a firm shake. "It's nice to meet you as well, Jane Montgomery. How goes the visit so far? Have you adjusted to the time difference?" As he anticipates her answer, he slides back into the booth, patting the seat beside him and indicating that Piper should utilize it.

Jane sits across from the couple and smooths her skirt. "I was pretty jet-lagged yesterday, but I'm feeling much better today. I was telling Piper that I'm excited to try this place. The woman I flew into Redmond with suggested I check it out."

"Yes, well, I heard you're an English major and thought you'd appreciate it." He lifts a short glass filled halfway with amber liquid, ice cubes clinking as he takes a small sip. "The drinks here have clever names. This is an F. Scotch Fitzgerald, but I'm also a big fan of the Gin Eyre."

"My go-to is the Are You There, God? It's Me, Margarita," Piper volunteers with a grin.

Jane laughs and picks up the cocktail menu residing on the table. Though she's drawn to the Tequila Mockingbird (simply because she loves the book *and* the play on words), what she opts for is a S(ide)carlett Letter. A waiter appears to take their orders, provides them with dinner menus, and quickly runs through the evening's specials: a porterhouse topped with crab imperial and known as Great Expectations; A Clockwork Orange, which consists of baked orange roughy served with a twelve-bean salad; and the Count of Monte Cristo Sandwich.

When the waiter departs, Jane studies the short stack of books at the end of the table: *Dracula, The Virgin Suicides, Jurassic Park, The Cider House Rules,* and *Practical Magic.* Atop them is a candle, its flame flickering and dancing. "There's a borrowing card in the back of each one," Piper informs her, "so if something piques your interest, you're allowed to take it with you. The same is true of the books running along the back wall."

It's a clever idea. Jane wishes Philadelphia had a restaurant like this one.

Max takes another sip of his drink and clears his throat. "So," he begins, "I hear you work as a copy editor. Is that right?"

"It is," she confirms, "and I hear you defend folks accused of crimes."

"I do, yes. It's a job with an oft-negative connotation, I know, but—"

"Atticus Finch was a defense attorney and he's one of literature's greatest heroes."

The smile that lights Max's face is one of surprise. "You know, I think I like this one," he says just loudly enough for Jane to hear, leaning in to speak the words into his fiance's ear. "It seems you've made a wise choice in selecting her as your maid of honor."

"I agree," Piper says, meeting her cousin's gaze. "I probably should've put you in charge of my bachelorette party, too. It just seemed a lot to ask since you live on the opposite side of the country. I didn't want to put you in that position. I mean, you don't know which bars around here are decent and which ones are lame." She sighs and accepts the cocktail that's just been delivered to the table. "As it is, I won't be surprised if the night ends up being lame anyway."

Jane arches her brows as she plucks the twist of orange rind from the side of her glass. She places this on a napkin and wonders, "Why do you think it'll be lame? What's the plan?"

Since so many friends and family members will be traveling from out of state, many of the wedding festivities will occur in a bit of a whirlwind toward the end of the week. A bachelorette party is scheduled for Thursday night; manicures, pedicures, and a rehearsal dinner for Friday; makeup, hair, and mimosas on Saturday morning; and a massive reception following the couple's "I do's" later that afternoon.

It seems impossible that the bachelorette party won't be fun. Piper is relatively simplistic when it comes to expectations for having a good time: margaritas, spicy food, dancing, and maybe some karaoke. To deviate from this combination would be both foolish *and* completely unnecessary.

A second member of the waitstaff appears and places a long wooden board on the table. It offers a variety of cheeses, several different types of crackers, a tiny jar of fig jam, and a small dish of adorably miniature eggs.

47

"The Stinky Cheese Man and Other Fairly Tasty Quails," she says with a completely straight face. "Your waiter will be back in a moment to take your orders."

"I took it upon myself to request a starter," Max explains. "A cheeseboard seemed a safe bet."

Jane thanks him and helps herself to a cracker layered with a smear of brie and a dollop of jam. As she pops it into her mouth, she waits for additional details regarding Thursday's outing. Piper glances discreetly at Max and absently touches her cheek. There'd normally be a faint smattering of freckles there beneath her right eye, an asymmetrical constellation similar to the painted-on freckles of Cabbage Patch Kids. Now, however, the blemish is invisible. Jane wonders if her cousin has intentionally covered it with makeup; she thinks back to yesterday and the day before, trying to remember if the haphazard flecks had been disguised then as well.

"So," Piper finally begins, her tone hesitant. "I put Marta in charge of the bachelorette party—"

"And Marta is...?"

"My older sister," Max provides. "She's a good person, and means well, but sometimes misses the mark when it comes to recognizing what's best for a particular situation. She has a tendency to... Hmm. How do I say this nicely?"

"Put herself first," Piper says flatly, "which is why we're going to the spa."

"The spa?" Jane confirms.

"The spa," Piper repeats. "I mean, don't get me wrong: facials, mud baths, and massages *sound* like a nice time, but that's not really the point of a bachelorette party, is it? I've always thought of it as a last hoorah. Like, I don't want to dance with other men or anything... but I *was* hoping to dance."

Jane delicately picks up one of the hard-boiled quail eggs and bites it in half. It tastes, she's surprised to find, almost exactly like a chicken egg. "Did you *tell* Marta you were hoping to go dancing?"

"No."

"Why not?"

"Well, because I don't want to hurt her feelings."

It seems to Jane that *Max* should be the one to communicate this dilemma to his sister, but rather than come to his fiance's defense, he takes Piper's hand in his and says calmly, "It will all be fine. Think how relaxed you'll feel afterward. You and your friends will be renewed and rejuvenated just in time for the wedding! And there will be dancing at the reception. If you'll let me, I'll spend the entire evening with you on the dance floor."

The smile tugging at the corners of Piper's mouth is less than convincing. "I know," she says. "I know it'll be fine. It's only one day, right? Jeez... How much of a brat am I to complain about receiving spa treatments at one of the hoitiest-toitiest places in Bend?" She shakes her head, dismissing the topic of conversation all together, and says brightly, "We should figure out what we want to eat! Our waiter will be back any minute."

JONNY.

Monday, 2:45a.m. (EDT)

Due to Alex's work schedule and his upcoming time in the air, Jonny knows he won't be able to readily communicate with his girlfriend for quite some time. He also knows the odds of her answering her cell while in the middle of a shift aren't promising. For this reason, he quickly scrolls through his contacts until he finds the number for the veterinary hospital. Then, jabbing the call button with his thumb, he lifts the flip phone to his ear and listens as the tinny sound of ringing filters through the line.

"Moonglow Emergency Clinic," someone answers almost immediately. "This is Jess."

"Jess, this is Jonny. Is Alex around?"

"Oh! Hey, Jonny. Yeah... she's here somewhere. Let me see if I can track her down."

"Thank you."

He waits, listening to instrumental music that's occasionally interrupted by informative details about keeping pets healthy: "Heartworm disease is a serious and potentially fatal condition that can be prevented by..."

"Parasites are not necessarily visible to the naked eye. This is why it's recommended that your pet have a stool sample checked every..."

"In the state of North Carolina, it is mandatory that all cats, dogs, and ferrets be vaccinated for rabies by the age of—"

This last bit of trivia is halted midstream. A second later, Alex's voice comes across the line. "Jonny?" She sounds a bit breathless. "Is everything okay?"

"What? Oh, yeah. I'm just... sitting here on the plane, waiting for takeoff. I figured I'd give you a call since my phone'll probably be off for the majority of the day. You sound kind of winded. What were you doing?"

"Honestly? I was about to change my scrub top. We had a hit-by-car come in a little while ago—a Cane Corso named Ralphie; he's built like a bulldozer and is gonna be fine—but he got scared when Dr. Ellison examined him, which caused him to express his anal glands all over me. I reek at the moment. Be glad you're far, far away." She laughs, the sound playful and musical. "So you're on the plane?"

"Yep."

"And your next stop is...?"

"Chicago, with a four-hour layover."

"Yikes! What're you gonna do with yourself?"

"I brought a book."

"Right, okay. But what're you gonna do with yourself?"

Jonny laughs. It's true that he's not an avid reader, but he *has* been known to pick up a nonfiction text every now and again. He's always meant to read *The Devil in the White City* and is determined to make a dent in it while soaring across the country. "Worst-case scenario?" he says, playing along. "I'll grab a beer and maybe make a new friend at one of the airport bars. Best-case scenario? I'll learn some new information about H. H. Holmes and the World's Fair."

Alex gasps. "You packed the Erik Larson book I gave you two Christmases ago?!"

"I sure did."

"Aww, I'm proud of you, Jonny!"

"Imagine how proud you'll be if I actually read it."

A *ding* sounds above him and a glowing seat-belt indicator flashes overhead.

"Hey," Jonny says softly, "I should get going. The flight attendant's about to go through his spiel and I need to turn off my phone. I'll call you when I get to Artie's, okay?"

"Okay. Have fun, sweetie."

"I will. Love you, Al."

"Love you too."

Jonny ends the call, powers down his cell, and slips the device into his pocket as a young man wearing a navy suit and an orange tie stands in the aisle and expertly projects his voice. "Ladies and gentlemen, welcome aboard Flight four-D-three with service from Charlotte to Chicago. We are currently second in line for takeoff and expect to be in the air in approximately five minutes' time. We ask that you please fasten..."

As he drones on, Jonny turns to the left and stares out the window, pondering for at least the thousandth time whether he's making a foolish decision. But when he lowers his lids and once again transports himself to that hole-in-the wall restaurant, his thoughts turn to Piper's emerald eyes and the sound of her voice as she'd curiously posed, "Have you ever wondered if people see colors the same way? Like, what if my red is your blue? Think about how many things would look so completely foreign!"

"Like flags," Jonny had said. "France's flag would be backwards."

Piper had looked at him, nibbling a chip and narrowing her eyes. "France, huh? It seems odd that's your go-to. I would've expected you to first comment on the American flag."

"Yeah, well... I'm a worldly guy."

"Oh, yeah?"

"Yeah."

"How so?"

Jonny'd wrapped a hand around his half-empty beer and spun the glass on its coaster, trying to act nonchalant. "I teach global studies," he remembers saying, "to eighth graders. Wouldn't you say that makes me kind of worldly?"

"Not as worldly as a world traveler," she'd laughed. "I thought you were going to tell me you're a photographer for *National Geographic* or something like that."

"A photographer? Nah. Just a history teacher." He'd taken a sip of his beer, then asked, "Why'd you assume I was a photographer?"

"I think I was projecting," Piper had responded. "I love photography and I guess... Well, I don't know. I guess I was secretly hoping you did too."

"I don't *dislike* it! I'm just not someone with a lot of talent when it comes to the arts."

"Really? That's surprising."

"It is?"

"You look as though you'd be the artsy type," she'd informed him. "It's your eyes, I think. They're soulful. Artists always have soulful eyes."

Jonny remembers this now and wonders if the mysterious Piper from Radio Park has been able to pursue her dream of becoming a photographer. He hopes that she has and makes a mental note to peruse the Yellow Pages once he lands in Oregon. Perhaps something will pop out at him. Perhaps there will be contact information for a business called Piper's Pictures and his search will be over. He takes a deep breath and crosses his fingers, hoping this is the case.

"Smoking is prohibited for the duration of the flight," the steward continues. "Thank you for choosing Augusta Airlines. Please enjoy your time in the clouds."

JANE.

Sunday, 11:58p.m. (PDT)

Kai raps a knuckle against the door of Jane's bedroom, the sound soft and hollow. When he peeks inside, he lifts a single brow and asks simply, "Thoughts?"

"The ambience was amazing, the cocktails were clever, and my pasta—Campanelle with a Chance of Meatballs—was delicious. It came with a side salad that had the most interesting dressing. Whisky-walnut. Have you had it before?"

"I have, yeah. It's good. And I'm glad you dug The Library, but when I asked about your thoughts, I was asking about your thoughts regarding *Max*. Like, what's your first impression of him?"

"Oh."

Kai narrows his eyes. "Oh?"

"I mean," Jane begins, not quite sure where to steer the sentence. She places the book she'd been reading face down on the bed beside her and pulls her knees to her chest. "He was—"

"Don't say 'nice.'"

"—nice."

They both laugh as Jane insists, "But he *was* nice!"

"Yeah, yeah. Whatever." Kai leans against the door jamb and slides his hands into the pockets of his khakis. "Listen... I know it's late, but do you have any interest in having a beer with me on the porch? I brought home a crowler of this tasty pale ale we started making—it's kind of fruity, kind of hazy—and I was gonna drink it before I went to bed. We were real busy at the brewery and I need to unwind before calling it a night."

Jane's already brushed her teeth and changed into pajamas. She's tired, but she *would* like to communicate with her cousin about Max. If she's being honest, she isn't sure how she feels about him, and from Kai's cryptic comments, it seems like he might not be either. "Sure, I'll split a crowler of beer with you. Let me scrounge up a hoodie and I'll meet you down there, okay?"

"Sounds like a plan. See you in a minute."

Monday, 12:36a.m. (PDT)

"I'm not a fan," Kai says matter-of-factly. "I just... I don't trust him, I guess. He's too pretty."

"Too pretty?" This seems a rather hypocritical observation seeing as the young man sitting across from her, with his dark hair and bright green eyes, looks as though he could just as easily model for Abercrombie and Fitch as tend bar at the Terrible Terrier. "You must have a stronger reason than that. What is it about him you don't like, Kai?"

"He's condescending," comes the response. "He thinks he's better than other people because he comes from money and has a law degree. And he, like, doesn't *get* Piper. He doesn't appreciate her creativity like he should. And sure, he acts all chivalrous or whatever, but it's not like he actually ever comes to her defense. He's real... manipulative, I guess? He's always twisting things around and making her think in ways she's never thought before."

Jane, sitting on the floor of the porch and leaning against the rail, crosses her legs and takes a sip of her beer. "Give me an example," she requests. "Be more specific."

"He wants her to stop working. Has she told you that?"

"What? No."

"Yeah. Max comes from this old-school belief that women are meant to stay home all day, cleaning and preparing dinner, while he goes off and earns a paycheck."

"Wait. Max actually *said* that?"

Kai glowers into his pint glass. "No, not in so many words. But it's what's gonna happen. Just watch. It's how he grew up. His dad's a lawyer and his mom's a housewife. Neither one of his sisters has a real career. The older one's married to a surgeon; she doesn't work. The younger one's dating a pharmacist; she has a part-time gig selling expensive clothes at some lofty shop downtown—"

"Lofty?"

Jane giggles, which earns a shy smile from Kai. "I just don't like him." The statement is blunt and honest. "Do you?"

"Tonight was the first time I met him, and we were only together for a few hours. But, I mean... I can see what you're saying. Pipe told me about the plans for her bachelorette party and—"

"At the spa? Yeah. That's exactly what I'm saying. Piper isn't a spa girl."

"I know. So the thing that bothered me, I guess, was that Max defended his sister. Marta, right?"

"Yeah."

"Okay, so... he opted to defend Marta rather than volunteer to talk to her about switching up the agenda. I thought that was kind of lame." She takes a sip of her beer and holds it in her mouth, allowing the carbonation to fizz at the back of her nose until the tickle is too persistent and she's forced to swallow. "I didn't even ask how many people are participating on Thursday. Do you know?"

"Marta, obviously, and Max's younger sister Maude. She's, like, the same age as Piper."

"Oh. So how old is Max?"

"Um... thirty-eight?"

Though the answer is formed as a question, it's voiced in a way that implies disbelief.

Coincidentally, disbelief is exactly what Jane is feeling. "Hold on. For real? Max is *eleven years older* than Piper?"

"Yep."

"Damn."

Kai nods knowingly and leans back in his seat, setting the rocking chair in motion. "So... Marta, Maude, Gabby, Reese, and Lauren. Gabby and Reese are high school friends; Lauren's a college buddy. There are seven of you in all. If you count Piper, I mean."

"And Max has six groomsmen?"

"Two guys from his firm and three guys he went to school with. And me."

"You made the cut, huh?"

"I wish I hadn't. The bachelor party was terrible. I mean, *Max* loved it... but I sure didn't."

Jane sets her glass beside her and hides her hands in the pocket of her sweatshirt. Despite the dry heat that had warmed the day, the night is chilly. "What'd you do?"

"Flew to Vegas for the weekend."

"Are you kidding?"

"Nope."

"So Max had an entire *weekend* to spend with his pals, doing whatever he wanted, and Piper gets a *spa day*, which is so *not* her style?"

"That's what I mean, Janie. He doesn't get her. At all. And he doesn't stick up for her when she needs sticking up for. I legit wish they weren't getting married." He takes a long swig of his beer and the speed of his rocking intensifies. "He's not the right guy for her."

Sighing, Jane leans her head against the slats of the railing and closes her eyes. "Yeah... I'm starting to agree with you."

JONNY.

Monday, 6:22a.m. (CDT)

The strange thing about airports is that when one is in them, time comes to a standstill.

Not a *complete* standstill. It's obviously important to be aware of departure times so appropriate gates can be reached before takeoff, but hours and minutes mean something different in airports. This is probably why Jonny doesn't feel especially awkward about requesting a Guinness to accompany his omelet and toast. He's been up since yesterday, so even though his stomach is craving breakfast, the rest of his body feels as though it's already put in a full day's worth of work. "Five o'clock somewhere, right?" he says to the man perched on the barstool beside him.

"Ain't that the truth."

The voice is deep and gritty-sounding, as if its owner had started smoking while still in the womb. A yellowish tinge and the thick consistency of his nails indicate this may be the case. "Just flew in from Salt Lake. Got two hours to kill and figured, 'Heck. Might as well kill 'em with a drink in my hand.'" He lifts his vodka tonic to further emphasize this belief.

"Where're you headed?" Jonny wonders. He'd planned to pass the time reading more about Holmes and his polygamist tendencies, but a bit of small talk with a stranger will work just as well.

"Home to New York. Got a daughter out west I was visitin' with. Spent the week with her. Just had a baby, she did. Little girl. Named her Loretta, if you can believe it. Loretta Beatrix Candleford. Now ain't that a name?" When he chuckles, the sound is phlegmy and moist. "Cute little bugger all the same, though. Gonna call her Lo. I kinda like that."

Jonny nods and picks up his beer, resting his right thumb upon the harp embossed there on the glass. "Is she your first grandchild?"

"First grand*daughter*," he clarifies, "but I got me three grandsons back home. Twins, and then an older boy." He sips his cocktail and adds, "The twins are a lot. Goin' on three years old now and already turnin' their parents prematurely grey." With nicotine-stained fingers, he squeezes his lime for the second time, then wonders, "What about you? Headin' east or west, north or south?"

"West."

"Whereabouts?"

"Oregon. Radio Park."

"Never heard of it."

"It's not far from Bend. I've got a buddy who lives out there. We went to college together."

"Is that right?"

Jonny refrains from mentioning the real reason he's headed west. If Owen thinks the mission is crazy, he can only imagine the opinion of a complete stranger. But what he'd *prefer* to talk about is the smattering of freckles that had existed just underneath Piper's right eye... and the way she'd struggled to pronounce the word "brewery."

"It's just a hard word for me," she'd said. "That repetition of *r* sounds paired with a *w*. I struggle. It's unfortunate, too, because Radio Park has a *lot* of brew-er-ies." The word, each time she'd spoken it, had been broken down into three distinct syllables. "I also have a tough time saying…" But rather than speak the vocabulary aloud, she'd pulled a pen from her purse and used it to scribble *s-i-x-t-h* on a cocktail napkin. Her handwriting had slanted to the right, the *s* more of a squiggle than a letter.

"Sixth?" Jonny'd confirmed, pronouncing the word with zero difficulty.

Piper had rolled her eyes in exasperation. "Yeah, alright. But who pairs an *x* with a *-th*? And then to put an *s* in front of the whole thing…? It's dumb. The whole concept is such a poorly thought-out grouping of letters."

For reasons he doesn't fully understand, Jonny would love to share this memory with the nameless man seated beside him, but he's only two sips into his Guinness and not yet inebriated enough to throw inhibition to the wind. So he bites down on the story, swallowing it with a bite of omelet before turning back to his drinking partner and prompting, "So… a new granddaughter. How old is she?"

Ansel.

For the remainder of Sunday, the needle of the compass tattooed on Ansel's right wrist had continued to drift eastward. This morning, however, the narrow indicator has swiveled around to veer south. It could mean anything: a continent or country, a state or city. For some reason, though, he suspects he's meant to travel to the southern section of Radio Park.

"Any interest in accompanying me to town?" he asks when Jane eventually ventures downstairs. "I have an order I need to drop off and would be willing to take you to lunch afterward. Unless you and Piper already have plans, that is."

His niece, clad in a pair of plaid pajama bottoms and a ribbed tank, stifles a yawn as she pads over to examine the coffee pot on the counter. It's empty. "I need caffeine," she says. "Kai and I were up really late last night. Assuming I go with you, can we stop for coffee along the way?"

"Of course."

"At one of the little huts?"

"Whatever you want, Janie-girl."

She smiles. "Okay. Do I have time for a quick shower?"

"There's absolutely no rush. Come find me in the barn when you're ready."

10:11a.m. (PDT)

Already, the temperature is approaching ninety. The sun's rays warm Ansel's back as he crosses the lawn, sandy soil coating his shoes. Despite the heat, Sophie has propped open one of the barn's doors, and as he approaches, the air grows progressively cooler. "Expecting to make a fair profit from that landscape with the poppies, are you? Is that why we're now cooling the entire street?"

"Hmm?" his wife wonders, spinning to face him. She wears her hair down today, a curtain of white-flecked-darkness that falls nearly to her waist. In her hands is a large canvas depicting the river that runs through Radio Park. It's an older piece—something she completed last summer—but from the empty spots on the wall and the additional oil paintings propped against a nearby table, it seems she's in the process of rearranging the art. "Oh. I'm sorry," she says as her gaze drifts toward the open door. "Wallace couldn't decide if he wanted to be inside or outside and I was tired of catering to his incessant mews. He's made his decision, though."

Wallace, a large grey tabby with a notched ear and a stubby tail, sprawls beside the cash register. When he catches Ansel's eye, his lips part in a silent greeting before he shields his face with a paw. The cat adopted the Fergusons three years ago when he'd meandered onto their property and decided to stay. At first, he contented himself with a hideaway under the front porch steps, but as the weather grew colder, he'd weaseled his way into the shop. If it weren't for Kai's allergies, he'd be a welcome member of the household, but the poor kid's eyes water like crazy and sneezing fits ensue whenever he's around felines for too long. This doesn't stop Kai from smothering Wallace with affection—he just has to do it with treats instead of snuggles... and follow each interaction with a shower.

Ansel closes the door, then heads back to his studio. "I'm gonna drop some art at Rufus Longfellow's place. Janie's coming with me. I told her we'd get lunch afterward. Does that sound alright to you?"

"Sounds lovely," Sophie assures him.

As he wraps the frames in an old quilt, his wife sings along with the radio, her notes never quite aligning with what the musicians are playing. It isn't until the off-key serenade comes to an abrupt halt that he realizes Jane has entered the shop. Her voice carries back to him, though he can't make out what it is she's saying. When he returns to the front of the barn, however, he finds that she's been recruited to hold canvases against the wall while Sophie stands back and considers possible new locations. "Up just a little," she instructs. "Now maybe an inch to the right."

Jane obliges, fulfilling each of her aunt's requests. "I like this one," she says of the winding river. "It reminds me of the time both our families went tubing. I wouldn't mind doing that again."

"Well, this week is certainly hot enough for tubing," Sophie muses. "Tell Piper you'd like to go. Or Kai. I'll bet either one of them would be willing to take you." She lifts the painting from Jane's hands and lines it up beside the others. "I'll keep fiddling with these. You two have fun in town. Don't let Rufus talk you into buying a reptile."

"Um... okay?"

The look of sheer confusion on Jane's face causes Ansel to laugh out loud. "I'll explain that comment in the car," he tells her. "Come on."

JONNY.

"Are you going to Oregon too?" asks a little voice.

Jonny turns to glance at his traveling companion. She has blonde hair worn in a long braid, a bald doll baby that sits on her lap, and an inquisitive purse to her lips. The child looks to be no more than four or five. He grins at her, but before he's able to answer, her mother leans over and explains, "Everyone is going to Oregon, baby. We all got on the plane in Phoenix, Arizona, and we'll all exit the plane in Redmond, Oregon. Remember?"

The little girl nods in acknowledgement of the explanation, but doesn't pull her eyes from Jonny. "So you're going to Oregon too?"

"Yep, I am."

"What's your name?"

"Jonny. What about you?"

"Cory."

"Short for Coriander," her mother explains. "Her father thought it would be cute to name our children after herbs. He's a chef; he's always experimenting in the kitchen."

"So you've got more than one child?"

"I have two brothers!" Cory offers. "Sorrel is seven and Basil is six. They stayed home, but Mommy and me were on a girls' weekend to see my Aunt Roxy." She beams, apparently proud to have been included in such an adult-like outing, and Jonny can't help but laugh.

"Is Oregon home for you guys?"

The question is directed at Cory's mother, who puts down her magazine and smiles. "We live in Bend. Are you familiar with it?"

"That's actually where I'm going. Well... Bend *and* Radio Park. I've got a buddy who lives in Bend, so I'll be staying with him, but I'm hoping to spend a good bit of time in Radio Park as well. I've got sort of a... a mission, I guess you'd call it?"

"A secret mission?" Cory wonders, her voice a theatrical whisper. "Or can you tell us?"

Jonny had consumed two pints of Guinness while passing time in O'Hare and then followed it up with a potent double IPA to kill time during his layover in Phoenix. He'd still been full from his breakfast and therefore hadn't ordered lunch, so he's feeling a bit buzzed at the moment. His tongue is looser than usual. "I can tell you," he decides. "Since you guys are familiar with the area, you might even be able to help."

Cory's mother quirks a brow, looking intrigued.

With nearly two more hours to be spent in the sky, Jonny starts at the story's beginning. He shares some of the details regarding his initial trip west—the one that had occurred between college and the world of adulthood—and provides a bit of commentary about his visit to the Grand Canyon. "I was in the middle of a ten-mile hike," he remembers, "when my shoe fell apart. The sole just... peeled off. I ended up tearing off one of the sleeves from my t-shirt and using it to tie everything together."

Both Cory and her mother (Natalie, he learns somewhere near the middle of the conversation) widen their eyes in amazement when they hear this anecdote.

Hoping his traveling companions may be of some assistance in his quest, Jonny describes what Piper looks like—her unbelievably green eyes and her straight, dark hair—and relays her interest in photography. He mentions the restaurant she'd told him about, Olé, and is pleasantly surprised to learn that it's still in business. "I think I mentioned my husband's a chef," Natalie says. "As a result, he's friendly with most of the area's restaurant owners. Olé's a fun spot. If you have time, check it out while you're in Radio Park. And while you're in Bend, you should definitely give Thyme Waits for No One a try."

"That's your husband's place?"

She nods. "His specialty is flatbreads."

"*Fancy* flatbreads," Cory pipes up, "with herbs like sorrel and basil and coriander on top!"

Jonny chuckles, then goes on to share the other details he remembers about Piper. Not everything. He doesn't deem it important to comment on the moon-shaped dimple that had appeared to the left of her mouth each time she'd smiled, or the way she'd begun to speak with a slight lisp after her third margarita. But he *does* make it a point to mention her love of photography and her father's tattoos. "That doesn't sound like anyone you know, does it?"

Natalie shakes her head apologetically. "If Piper's in her late twenties, we're more than ten years apart, so I'm not surprised that we run in different circles. She doesn't sound familiar to me; I'm sorry." She chews her bottom lip for a moment and runs a hand down her daughter's braid. Then, with an expression Jonny isn't quite able to read, she adds, "There *is* something familiar about the man with tattoos, though. It may be nothing, but..."

On its own, Jonny's back straightens. He blocks out the whoosh of air coming from the circular vent above him and ignores the steady rumble of the plane's engines. "But what?" he prompts.

"Years ago, I can remember taking a piece of art into Radio Park to have it framed. I don't remember the name of the shop *or* the name of the man who did the work for me, but he and his wife rented a little storefront downtown. She was an artist too—landscapes, mostly, I believe—and *he* was a bit of an illustrated man. Incredibly friendly, but his appearance was intimidating. Tall, muscular... he had a big beard and a bald head." Natalie pauses, trying to recall more details. "I'm not sure if they had kids; it's entirely possible. Oh... I *wish* I could remember the name of the frame shop. It's just... it's not coming to me. I'm sorry."

"No, it's okay!" Jonny assures her. "What you've given me is a place to start. A frame shop in downtown Radio Park. I can work with that." He exhales slowly, relaxing his posture and melting into his seat. For the first time since leaving Moonglow, North Carolina, he feels the tiniest bit hopeful.

JANE.

Monday, 10:48a.m. (PDT)

The hut is closed. This becomes apparent as soon as Ansel steers his truck into the parking lot. The window is shuttered and the menu is absent. "We can try someplace else. Either another coffee hut or, if you don't tell your Aunt Sophie, we can drive over and check out that new spot on Bender Boulevard. We'll be passing it anyway."

Only slightly disappointed, Jane agrees to this change of plan. Ultimately, the goal is caffeine; it shouldn't really matter what type of establishment the caffeine comes from.

Ansel hops back on the main road and follows it into town, avoiding weekday traffic by navigating less-populated side streets. When he comes to the intersection of George Street and Bender Boulevard, he turns left. "That's where Kai works," he says, pointing to a small brewery. The building sports vertical wooden siding. A large dog, black in color and cut from metal, sits to the left of the door. Overhead, displayed on a narrow sign, are the words "Terrible Terrier Brewing Co."

"What kind of terrier is it named after?" Jane wonders, thinking of Dennis and his short little legs. With the exception of Airedales, she can't come up with a breed that stands as tall as the one depicted in front of the brewery.

"A Black Russian, I believe, named Boris. Kai tells me he spends a lot of time there, socializing with customers and eating the crusts of their sandwiches. The few times I've been in, though, Boris hasn't been around." He guides the pickup into an available spot, parallel parks like a pro, shuts off the engine, and pockets the key. "Ready?"

Jane stands on the sidewalk and considers the building in front of her. Its exterior is comprised of browns: brown siding the color of cappuccino, a brown banister the color of espresso, brown trim reminiscent of caramel. A yellow door provides a cheerful welcome; purple flower boxes host an assortment of red, pink, and orange annuals. A round sign hangs from the eaves above: "Cup o' Mud Buzz." The apostrophe is a coffee bean with wings, its stripes yellow and brown.

"It may not be a hut," Jane says, "but this place is adorable!"

Ansel chuckles and leads the way up the porch steps, holding the door for his niece. "After you."

Stepping into the shop is like stepping into a milky latte. The aroma is heavenly—nutty and rich and strong—and the walls, with the exception of one, are a creamy brown. Adding a pop of color, a single expanse has been papered in purple paisley. None of the furniture actually matches, but everything has been painted a shade of orange: tangerine tables, peach-fuzz chairs, stools the same hue as a sunrise.

A tall counter runs along the back wall; a chalkboard menu hangs above it. "This is on me, Unc. What would you like?"

When at home, Jane knows her uncle typically takes his coffee black, but she also recalls that he's been known to branch out when visiting a place that specializes in caffeinated beverages. Today, she's pleased to discover that he's in the mood for an iced caramel latte. "And I'll have the same," she tells the barista, "only make mine hot."

"You got it!"

The woman sets to work on their drinks, grinding the beans and steaming the milk. It's a noisy process, but she raises her volume and manages to be heard over the commotion. "Are you folks from around here?"

"I am," Ansel informs her, "but Janie's visiting from Pennsylvania."

"Oh, yeah?" The barista—her name tag indicates that she goes by Lara—fills a cup with ice and pours the ingredients over the cubes. "I've got a brother in Pennsylvania. He runs a coffee shop in a tiny town called Lake Caywood. You've probably never heard of it."

Jane's heart quickens. She certainly *has* heard of Lake Caywood. "You're kidding. That's where I went to college! Please do not tell me your brother is Joe Abbott."

Lara laughs, and even before she confirms that this is the case—that the world really and truly *is* incredibly small—the similarities between the siblings become strikingly apparent. Lara, every bit like her brother, looks as if she's just walked off a beach in California. Her hair is golden, her skin is sunkissed, and her eyes are a bright and clear blue. "You know Joe?" she confirms. "That's hilarious!"

Jane considers mentioning that she also knows Joe's identical twin, and that Chet Abbott had actually dated her good friend Lucy Campbell for a couple of years, but because the relationship had ended rather awkwardly, and also because Chet had moved home to California shortly following the split, she refrains from bringing this up. The connection to Joe is enough.

Lara places a lid on the iced latte and slides it across the counter. Then she does the same to the hot beverage and passes it to Jane. Her eyes crinkle as she smiles. "What're the odds, right? Two worlds colliding... Life sure is a funny thing."

11:31a.m. (PDT)

Rufus Longfellow is a short and squat man with a mop of curls and a few missing teeth. As a result, the words that exit his mouth are often accompanied by a subtle whistle. "Nice to meet ya, Jane!" he exclaims once Ansel has made the necessary introductions. His hand, when he places it in hers, is dry and calloused.

"Nice to meet you too," Jane answers automatically, though she's not entirely sure she means it.

While her uncle unwraps the framed artwork he's brought along to drop off, she moves around the store, taking in the many reptiles in their aquariums. There are bearded dragons and green anoles and a leopard gecko the color of flames. Jane avoids the ball python with its banana-hued splotches, but does take a moment to marvel at a tortoise munching on a wedge of watermelon. Contained in a plastic pool, the shelled creature seems quite consumed by its meal, but when it catches sight of the woman peering down at it, the shriveled head swivels upward to consider its audience.

"That's Marvin," Rufus informs her. "He's five years old and loves kale more'n anyone I've ever met. Go on and pet 'im if you want to; he's real friendly."

Jane squats down and tentatively extends a hand, placing two of her fingers on the knobby divot between the tortoise's eyes. "Hi Marvin," she whispers. "You're kind of cute in your own funny way. D'you know that?"

"Oh, he knows it alright!" Rufus chuckles, coming over to stand behind her. "I tell 'im every day. He's the only fella in here not lookin' for a new family. Goes home with me each night, he does. Doc told me a few years back that I oughta cut red meat from my diet. High cholesterol, you know? Said what I oughta do is eat more fruits and vegetables, which is why I adopted Marvin. Russian torties are herbivores, so I figured if I was needin' to buy produce for him, I might be more inclined to buy some for m'self!"

"And has it worked?" Jane wonders.

"Maybe not as well as I would've liked," Rufus admits, "but it hasn't hurt any."

Near the door, Ansel tries to mask his grin. "Are you ready to grab lunch, Janie-girl? There's a little sandwich shop around the corner I think you might like. If we hurry, we should be able to beat the noontime rush."

Jane nods and gets to her feet, looping her bag over her shoulder. She waves goodbye to Marvin, then Rufus, and follows her uncle outside. The brilliant sunshine is almost as bright as the many lamps illuminating the reptile store had been. "He's an odd character," she notes, falling into step beside Ansel.

"'Odd' is definitely an understatement, but he's a nice man."

They cut down a sidestreet, passing a few local shops before coming upon a vintage theatre that only resembles a theatre because of the marquee overhead. "What's this place?" Jane wonders, pausing on the sidewalk to stare up at the sign. Rather than movie titles, band names are listed there in bold, red letters. She recognizes one of them in particular.

"The Post Press," Ansel answers. "They used to print newspapers here, but now it's a concert venue. We've had some fairly well-known artists come through this past year. Your Aunt Sophie and I saw Norman Greenbaum last September. It's cozy inside. Kind of intimate."

"Norman Greenbaum?" The name isn't a recognizable one. "Who's that?"

Placing a hand over his heart, Ansel feigns injury. "You're killing me, Janie," he sighs, and promptly begins singing. His voice is deep and rich—far better than her aunt's. For as much as Sophie enjoys music, she can't carry a tune to save her life.

"It doesn't sound familiar," Jane says, interrupting her uncle's serenade about dying and then spending the afterlife with Jesus.

"'Spirit in the Sky,'" he says in disbelief. "You're telling me you don't know 'Spirit in the Sky'?"

She shakes her head and points to the sign above her. "But I *do* believe you about the well-known artists. If the Post Press can get Flannel Lobster, then—"

"Who?"

Now it's Jane's turn to fix her uncle with an incredulous expression. "Unc. Really? They're, like, *all over* the radio right now."

"Name a song I might know."

"'Uptempo, Down.'"

He tilts his head to one side, runs a hand over his robust beard. "Nope. Not ringing a bell."

Jane rolls her eyes and clears her throat, sings the chorus that is currently being overplayed on airwaves across the nation: "*'Fast is fast and slow is slow; / You need both speeds to make life go. / Reprieves are nice, but so's gusto: / A minute down, then uptempo!'* Now... tell me you don't recognize that."

Ansel grins. "Yeah, alright. It may sound a little bit familiar." He places an arm across her shoulders and walks her under the marquee, leading her out the other side and farther down the street. "This little sandwich shop I'm taking you to? The chicken salad is incredible. Trust me."

ANSEL.

Monday, 12:18p.m. (PDT)

Although Ansel thinks of it as a sandwich shop, he supposes On the Side (thus named because of its sidestreet location *and* culinary specialty) is actually known for the dishes that accompany its main courses. In fact, an option exists to order only half a sandwich, wrap, or sub, which is fortunate since each entree automatically comes with three sides.

Jane takes her uncle's recommendation and orders a chicken salad wrap. Ansel does the same, pairing it with roasted potatoes, baked vegetables, and beets tossed with walnuts, blue cheese, and balsamic. They sit at a table for two that's positioned near the front window, Jane facing the Post Press and him looking in the opposite direction. The compass on his wrist tingles a bit, as if the needle is moving back to its original position. He wonders if this visit to the southern part of town has proven fruitful; short of experiencing an exceptionally delicious caramel latte, he can't think of anything especially notable that's occurred.

Jane is unusually quiet. Ansel watches her expression as she samples a stalk of marinated asparagus, knowing that if Piper were here, she'd comment on the fact that her cousin's urine will smell funny later.

"Hey, Unc? Can I ask you a question about Max's family?"

"Ask away. I'll do my best to give you an honest response."

Jane doesn't speak immediately, seemingly organizing her thoughts. She stares out the window for a moment, squinting toward the marquee advertising that band with some sort of crustacean in its name, until she gathers the courage to voice what's in her head. And then she wonders, "What're Max's sisters like? Specifically Marta. Is she someone who'd... I don't know. Would she be upset if plans were to change at the last minute?"

"Yes," Ansel says without hesitation. "Why are you asking?"

"Because of Piper's bachelorette party. I understand why she didn't ask me to plan it, but I should have offered. I'm feeling guilty about it. Sure, it would've been tricky to organize things while in Philadelphia—I totally get that—but at the same time... Well, we wouldn't be spending the day at a *spa*."

Ansel had been surprised when he'd found out his daughter placed her fiance's sister in charge of Thursday's festivities. He'd been equally surprised to eventually learn the details of those plans. "I hope the spa has margaritas," he jokes now, "because that's ultimately what Piper's going to want."

"That and dancing," Jane mutters. "I just... I don't know. I'd sort of like to take charge and make everything better. Piperfy the evening, if you will. But I also don't want to offend Marta; I know she put a lot of work into the plans she *did* put together."

Ansel bites his tongue. What he'd like to do is encourage his niece to seize control of the situation and arrange something that actually sounds like his daughter. On the other hand, he's been around Marta enough times

79

to realize that doing this could backfire terribly. Some women, he's come to find, can be petty creatures; the last thing he wants is for Piper to endure the silent treatment—or worse—from one of her bridesmaids on her wedding day. "I think," he says carefully, "if you attempt to alter Thursday's plans, there's a good chance you'll face some backlash from Marta. Whatever you come up with, it'll need to be more elaborate than what she already has in mind."

"What about the rest of the bridesmaids?"

Gabby and Reese, high school friends of his daughter, were frequent guests in the Fergusons' home. Ansel can't begin to count the number of times the girls had carried a boombox into the living room, cranked up the music, and conducted a dance party while dressed in their pajamas. He feels confident that they'd both prefer an evening of dancing. His interactions with Lauren have been more sporadic, seeing as she roomed with Piper while the two were away at college, but the limited contact he *has* had leads him to believe that she'd prefer a wild evening to a calm one. As for Max's younger sister...

"The only point of contention—other than Marta, that is—may come from Maude... but then again, she also might be fine with a switcheroo. I don't know her well at all, and my intuition could be completely inaccurate, but I haven't gotten the impression she's quite as *particular* as her sister. There's a good chance Marta may be your only obstacle."

Jane pulls her strawberry locks over her shoulder, twirling the ends around her right index finger as she ponders all that's been shared. After a long sip of iced tea, she meets her uncle's gaze and holds it. "Am I crazy for wanting to switch things up at the last minute?"

"Maybe a little," Ansel admits, "but I know the crazy comes from a good place."

She smiles and looks away, squinting again at that marquee down the street. In a voice barely audible over the diner's soundtrack of lunch conversations, she mutters, "I may have an idea, Unc. It probably won't amount to anything, but... we'll see. I'm gonna make a phone call when we get back to the house. 'Til then, just cross your fingers, alright?"

JONNY.

By the time Jonny's collected his luggage, rented a car, and driven from Redmond to Bend, the only thing on his mind is a nap.

"You look beat," Artie says when he meets his friend in the driveway. "I figured you would be. You've probably been up for over twenty-four hours straight."

"I honestly couldn't tell you," Jonny says, trying his best to mask a yawn. He's been in so many different time zones by this point that he no longer has any idea how long he's been awake. Looping his backpack over a shoulder, he lifts his suitcase and follows Artie up the walkway to the townhouse. The first thing he notices is the building's coloring: charcoal grey with rich, wooden accents. The second thing he notices is the structure's lack of gutters.

"Bend doesn't get enough rain to really warrant them," Artie explains when Jonny asks about it. Then he props the front door and ushers him inside.

The home is fairly new, with an open floor plan and modern appliances. Without asking, Artie leads the way to the kitchen and pulls two beers from the refrigerator, twisting off the caps and handing a bottle to his friend. Jonny accepts it graciously and takes a long sip.

"The master bedroom's off the living room, but the guest room's upstairs. You'll not only have your own bathroom, but there's also a balcony with a private entrance. I'll hook you up with a key." He leans against the kitchen counter and continues, "Since I left work kinda early today, I'll probably end up staying late tomorrow to make up the hours. That's cool, right? I figured it wouldn't be much of an issue since you've sorta got your own agenda."

"That sounds great, man. Like I said on the phone, I'm not expecting to be entertained."

"Alright, well... I *would* like to catch up. I get that you're pretty drained right now, but if you're up for it later, there's a place downtown that serves really hot wings and really cold beers. I thought we could grab dinner before calling it an early night."

"Perfect," Jonny manages around another yawn. "I may need a quick power nap first."

"Yeah, yeah. Of course. Let's get you situated and see how things pan out. If you're too tired—"

"Nah, I'll be fine."

"You sure?"

"Positive. I'll try out the bed, grab a quick shower, and we can maybe head out around six?"

Artie nods. "Sure thing, bud. Sounds like a plan."

Arturo Beltran has almond-colored skin, high cheekbones, a very pronounced nose, and dark hair that falls across his forehead. He's pretty in an unconventional way. In college, his nickname had been Baby, and at the time Jonny had assumed it was because he was a year younger than the rest of the guys they ran with. Now, however, he wonders if it had more to do with his effeminate mannerisms. Artie wipes his fingers after handling each wing; he uses his napkin to dab at the corners of his mouth. These are things that had slipped from Jonny's mind over the years, and witnessing the familiar gestures once again brings a smile to his lips. "I forgot what a tidy eater you are," he says, which causes Artie to grin right along with his pal.

Artie's home had been tidy as well. Clean towels waited in a stack on the bathroom sink, a fresh bar of soap resided in the shower, and the guest room itself carried the lemony aroma of furniture polish. The presentation impressed Jonny; he doubts he would have thought to make his own home quite as presentable before hosting a friend.

"So tell me about this mysterious woman you're trying to track down," Artie says. He dips a celery stalk in a small container of ranch dressing and crunches down on it. "I'm assuming you and Alex broke up. I'm sorta surprised the relationship lasted as long as it did."

Jonny quirks an eyebrow. Only once have Artie and Alex had the opportunity to spend time together, and it had been at a wedding. The setting wasn't ideal for getting to know an individual's true personality, so this particular comment comes as a bit of a surprise. "Why would you say that?"

"I don't know. She just struck me as someone who required more maintenance than what you'd typically be drawn to. You were the guy who never had clean underwear and was always wearing wrinkled shirts because you didn't fold your laundry when you took it out of the dryer. And Alex... Well, she just seemed to me like someone who wears a lot of makeup and always has her nails done. That's all. Maybe I'm totally off base." He shrugs and takes another bite of celery.

Jonny pulls a chunk of meat from a drumstick and dunks it in blue cheese, processing this.

The thing is, Alex *can* be a lot of work. She has a standing appointment every two weeks to have her nails done, and another standing appointment every five weeks to have her hair cut and colored. She spends a good thirty minutes on her makeup before ever leaving the house, she irons all of her clothes before putting them on, and her favorite type of gift to receive is silver with some sort of gemstone incorporated into the design. And yet, there have been so many times when she's come home smelling of anal glands and wearing scrubs smeared with feces and vomit. She's not *always* high maintenance; she can actually be quite down-to-earth about things.

Rather than visit the complexities of his relationship with Alex, Jonny decides to focus on Piper instead. He tells Artie about the conversation he'd had with Natalie on his flight from Phoenix to Redmond, describing the frame shop and asking if anything about the story rings any bells.

"I've never had to have anything framed," Artie says apologetically. "Sorry, bud."

Jonny hangs his head, trying hard not to feel defeated. "The frame shop is *still* a lead," he reminds himself. A lead that he'd only just learned about earlier today. To assume the first person he asked about it would know something is unrealistic. He'll stick with his original plan and check the Yellow Pages first thing tomorrow. And then, with any luck, he'll have a destination for when he drives into Radio Park for the first time.

JANE.

Monday, 9:56p.m. (PDT)

"Can I run something by you?"

Kai spins in his chair, turning his back to the computer on his desk. "Sure. What's up?"

"You know the band Flannel Lobster, right?"

"I do, yeah... because I'm not living under a rock." He grins to show that his sarcasm isn't meant to be offensive. "My mom loves that band, even though she can never remember their name. That new song that's out though? 'Uptempo, Down'? She sings it, like, *all the time.*"

Jane smiles and moves farther into his bedroom, plopping down on the mattress and leaning back against his pillows. They smell like boy: woodsy deodorant mingling with a hint of sleepy sweat. "They're gonna be in Radio Park later this week. On Thursday. What if I got tickets and made *that* the bachelorette party instead of a spa day? Would Piper be on board, do you think?"

"She'd love it, but that show's been sold out for months. The Post Press is tiny; it only holds a few thousand people. Tickets lasted for all of, like, fifteen minutes." The monitor behind him goes dark as neon squiggles start dancing across the screen. Kai scratches his stubbled cheek and gives his

87

cousin a sympathetic look. "It was a nice thought, though. Flannel Lobster would definitely trump the spa and no one—not even Marta Storm—could justify holding a grudge."

"The thing is," Jane begins, "I might still be able to snag us some tickets."

Kai appears skeptical. "How?" his eyes seem to ask, though his mouth offers nothing.

"Do you remember my friend Lucy?"

"Vaguely. She's blonde, isn't she? And worked at the bookstore with you?"

"Good memory!" Jane praises, and goes on to elaborate, "Something you maybe *don't* know is she dates the lead singer of Flannel Lobster."

Now an expression of intrigue occupies Kai's face. He tilts his head to one side, furrows his brow.

"I called him earlier this afternoon, just to find out if he'd be able to sneak us in. I had to leave a message because he didn't answer, but I'm hopeful he'll call me back. If he does—"

"You'll be a hero in the eyes of my sister!" Kai laughs and turns back around to face his computer. He wiggles the mouse, once again bringing the screen to life, and places his fingers on the keyboard. Typing so quickly as to create a *clickety-clack* chorus that echoes through the quiet room, he pulls up the band's website and visits a page of tour dates. "They're in Boise tonight, Seattle tomorrow, Portland on Wednesday, and here in Radio Park the following day. Thursday." He peers over his shoulder at Jane. "You really think you might be able to pull this off?"

Heat floods her cheeks. In actuality, the miracle will only occur if Sebastian Porter has the kind of influence she's hoping he does. "Supposing we're able to make this happen, how many tickets will we need? Eight?"

Kai shakes his head. "There are only seven of you."

"Right. And *you*."

His eyebrows shoot upward. "You want me to attend the bachelorette party?"

"I do if you're willing to help me plan this thing. You're my partner-in-crime!" Jane gives him a warm smile and waits for his response. She's never known her younger cousin to leave her in the lurch. Despite their seven-year age difference, the two have experienced some noteworthy adventures together... the most memorable being that time in Cape Cod when they'd confiscated the lobsters their families intended to boil for dinner, transported them down to the beach via backpacks and bicycles, removed the rubber bands from the crustaceans' claws, and released them to the wild. Piper had refused to participate that time, which meant she was allowed to watch the fireworks from the dock the following evening.

Jane and Kai had been forced to watch from the upstairs window of their beach house since the two of them had been grounded.

Chuckling softly, the young man lifts his shoulders in a show of agreement. "As long as I won't be expected to tease my hair or wear a dress, you can count me in. I'll see about switching my shift for Thursday; I'm sure I can find someone to cover for me."

"Okay, good. And I'll let you know if I hear from Bas."

"You'll let me know *when* you hear from him," Kai corrects. "We've gotta stay optimistic, cuz."

Tuesday, 3:02a.m. (PDT)

Charging on the nightstand beside her bed, Jane's phone buzzes in the wee hours of morning. The gentle vibration wouldn't typically wake her, but for some reason she stirs and fumbles for the glowing device. And there, on the screen, is a message from Flannel Lobster's frontman.

"Sorry it's late," Bas has written. "Got your message and wanted to let you know that shouldn't be a problem. I'll give you a call in the next day or two so we can finalize details. See ya Thursday!"

A shiver of anticipation courses through Jane's body as she closes her eyes and holds the covers tight beneath her chin. "Sorry, Marta," she whispers into the quiet room. "Your spa day just got canceled. We're going dancing instead."

JONNY.

Tuesday, 11:14a.m. (PDT)

Although he and Artie had planned for an early night, that's not at all what happened. After a dozen wings and two pints each, the men had returned to the townhouse and consumed the remainder of the six-pack in Artie's refrigerator, reminiscing about college and the ridiculous shenanigans they'd gotten into as teenagers. It is for this reason—the combination of jet-lag and a minor hangover—that Jonny doesn't open his eyes until the morning has all but reached its conclusion.

"Damn..." he muses, squinting at the dayglo digits on the clock beside his bed. "So much for making the most of my time here."

He runs a tongue over his gritty teeth, the taste in his mouth both sour and sweet. Stale beer mingling with the remnants of minty toothpaste. A groan escapes him as he throws back the covers and hoists himself into an upright position, then pads down the hall to the bathroom. He'll shower and change, he decides, and head into Radio Park for lunch.

Proving to be a helpful host, Artie left two brochures ("Beautiful Bend" and "A Visitor's Guide to Radio Park"), a map of central Oregon, and a phonebook on the kitchen table. Rather than peruse them at the house, Jonny had scooped everything into his arms and placed the materials on the passenger seat of his rental car, intending to read through them at whichever restaurant he ends up patronizing. He does, however, sneak a peek at his Radio Park literature, which lists The Bar as the city's oldest culinary establishment.

Centrally located amongst several law firms in town, the venue's original name, Charleston's, was rarely utilized; more often than not, the structure was simply referred to as The Bar. Attorneys sipped bourbon at The Bar while law students downed espresso and studied for the Bar.

Outside of what he's learned from *Law & Order*, Jonny Rockford knows very little about courtrooms and the people who work there, but he's intrigued by the fact that The Bar has been a part of Radio Park's history for such a substantial length of time. This is why he finds a parking spot, tucks Artie's phonebook under his arm, and heads inside.

The lighting is somber, the murmur of conversation faint. At first, he assumes the restaurant is simply experiencing a lull, but as his pupils adjust to the shadowy ambience and scan the room, he's surprised to find many of the tables are occupied and only a few seats remain open at The Bar's bar. He claims one and places his reading material on the counter in front of him, smiles when the bartender approaches with question marks dancing in her eyes. "Can I get you started with a drink?"

"Of your local beers, what do you recommend?"

"We've got a Deschutes pale ale on tap right now that's been really popular. I won't be surprised if the keg kicks later today, so if that sounds like something you'd be interested in checking out, I wouldn't procrastinate."

"Alright, I'll give it a try," Jonny agrees. "Can you hook me up with a menu too?"

"Sure can." She pulls one from beneath the counter and places it in front of him, tosses her ponytail over her shoulder, grabs a glass, and efficiently fills it with golden liquid. "Doesn't sound as though you're a native Oregonian," she notes, offering a discreet observation regarding his southern drawl. Her gaze lingers on the phonebook near his right hand, puzzling over but not asking about its presence.

"I'm here through Saturday, visiting a buddy from college."

"First time in Radio Park?"

"Yup. And you're my first stop."

"Wow! Did you choose The Bar because you're a lawyer?"

Jonny laughs. "I did *not*. I'm a history teacher, actually. I chose The Bar because this travel brochure," he says, tapping his finger against the colorful pamphlet, "says this place is the restaurant that's been here the longest. I figured I'd give it a try."

"We do have some killer salads," she informs him, "and our turkey club's not bad either. I'd recommend the chips instead of the fries, though; we make 'em here and they're really good."

After an unhealthy amount of artery-clogging food last night, the idea of fresh produce is appealing. He orders a southwest salad with blackened chicken, grilled chickpeas, and tangerine-chipotle dressing. The request earns praise from the bartender, who leaves him to sip his beer and study his reading materials in private.

Under the category of "Photographers/Photography," there are forty-one entries... only five of which are located in Radio Park. None of them reference anyone by the name of Piper, but Jonny does dogear the page so he can come back to it later. Then he flips backward in search of "Framing."

Only fifteen businesses are listed this time. He scans the boxed-off information, on the lookout for anything at all that reminds him of Piper or sounds vaguely reminiscent of her father. Not surprisingly, the mission proves fruitless. "Can I ask what it is you're looking for?" the bartender wonders as she slides a paper placemat and a bundle of utensils in front of him. "I'm only twenty-two, but I *have* lived here my whole life."

"Frame shops," Jonny says in a lackluster tone. "Specifically, I'm looking for a frame shop owned by a man with a lot of tattoos. Does that sound at all familiar?"

The young woman bites her lip and reluctantly shakes her head. "No, I'm afraid not. If you want, though, I can ask my manager. He's older than I am and might have a better idea of the businesses around town. I've never had to have anything framed, so..." She allows her words to trail away, not deeming it necessary to conclude the sentence.

"If you wouldn't mind, that'd be great. Thank you."

She disappears yet again and Jonny closes the phonebook. He's unsure what else to look under, so opens the Radio Park pamphlet instead. As he skims over statistics about the meandering river that runs through town and the Cascade Mountains located nearby, he attempts to block out the conversation happening only a few seats away. Though the trio of men isn't exactly loud, they *are* rowdier than the rest of the restaurant's clientele.

"Gonna be able to get some whenever you want," one of them says crassly. "That's a plus."

"Jesus, Dan..." the man in the middle groans. "That's not why I'm marrying her."

"Sure, yeah. I understand. It's more about arm candy, isn't it? She's a good-looking lady." This from the third member of the party.

"You guys are real assholes, you know it? Why the hell did I ask you to be in my wedding?"

Jonny turns ever so slightly, curious to catch a glimpse of these men who present themselves as distasteful and insensitive, but wanting to do so as inconspicuously as possible. From the corner of his eye, he observes their tailored suits and expensive ties. Two are white, one is multiracial; two sip whisky, one nurses a milky stout. They all, as far as Jonny is concerned, could accurately be described by the term "douchebag." Not that he's never had impure thoughts about Alex, but he'd certainly refrain from making uncouth statements in such a public venue. Whoever the middle man's fiance is, Jonny feels sorry for her.

1:34p.m. (PDT)

The manager appears just as Jonny fills his mouth with a big bite of salad. The timing is poor, to say the least, and the forty-something-year-old chuckles apologetically. "Go on and finish chewing," he says, his manner amicable. "I'll tell you what I know about tattooed men running frame shops in Radio Park and you can listen. How's that sound?"

Jonny bobs his head appreciatively.

The man rolls his shoulders and crosses his arms over his paunchy stomach. He has a bristly mustache that hangs low, concealing most of his upper lip. "Quite a ways back... must've been at least five years ago now, maybe more; you know how time has a tendency to blur. Well, there was a store over on Water Street that offered custom framing. The guy who ran it was impressively tall—I'll bet he was over six-and-a-half feet, no exaggeration—and he had more than a few tattoos. I want to say his name was Andrew." He cuts himself off, shaking his head. "Nah, that's not right. It was more unusual than that. Anders, maybe? Oh, I can't remember.

"Anyway, as far as I know, the business shut down and the owner moved away. But if you're looking to track him down, I'd recommend talking to a fellow by the name of Xavier Kinney. He's got a shop on Water as well—specializes in sporting goods—and might have an idea of where

Anders, or whatever his name was, eventually ended up. That's my recommendation."

Jonny swallows his food and follows it with a swig of beer. "Xavier Kinney?" he confirms. "Do you know what his store's called?"

"Hike-Camp-Repeat."

"And it's on Water Street?"

"That's right."

"Okay," Jonny says. "Thanks a lot. I'll check it out once I've finished my meal... which is really good, by the way."

The manager smiles. "I appreciate the compliment and will pass it along to the kitchen staff. Good luck with your search." He raps his knuckles twice against the bar before walking away, leaving Jonny to run through the conversation again as he stabs a tomato with his fork.

JANE.

Tuesday, 2:18p.m. (PDT)

Although Jane told Kai about Sebastian's text first thing this morning, she refrains from mentioning it to Piper. Until details are finalized, she's reluctant to share the news with anyone beyond her young partner-in-crime, but this is easier said than done. More than anything, she wants to inform her cousin of the new-and-improved bachelorette party.

"What aren't you telling me?" Piper asks now, pulling a bright yellow sundress from the rack and holding it against her torso. It's not a color Jane could ever pull off; her complexion is far too fair and her strawberry locks look orangey in contrast with the warm hue. Piper, however, would probably be able to don a burlap potato sack and still make it look good.

Jane does her best to appear innocently confused as she prepares to rebuff her cousin's question. "What do you mean? I'm not keeping anything from you."

"Eh... I don't know if I believe you. You've got that look."

"What look?"

"That look you sometimes get when you have a secret thought."

Flipping through a display of denim jackets, Jane says dismissively, "I don't have a secret thought, Pipe."

"Is it about Max?"

"No."

Piper puts the dress back where she found it and fixes her cousin with an unblinking look. "I haven't really had a chance to talk to you since Sunday night. What did you think of him? He's great, isn't he?"

"He's handsome," Jane agrees, but she's reluctant to gush. What she'd like to do is substantiate some of the information Kai has volunteered, but she doesn't want to go about it in a way that will be offensive. "And generous, too. It was nice of him to pick up the tab."

"Oh, well, of course! I mean, money's not really an issue for him."

"Because of his job, or because his family's so wealthy?"

Piper's cheeks turn uncharacteristically rosy. Her eye contact falters as she admits, "Both."

"Is that weird?"

"Is what weird? The fact that he's rich?"

"Yeah."

"Um... no?" She tilts her head to one side, dark hair cascading over her shoulder. A crease appears at the bridge of her nose as she puzzles over the question. "Do *you* think it's weird?"

"No, not necessarily."

"Then why'd you ask?"

"Because I was curious." Jane checks the price of a jacket, crinkles her nose at the unexpectedly high number, and returns the item to its rack. "I work as a copy editor, you know? And Marcus makes decent money as an accountant... but, I don't know. I just think it must be interesting to never have to worry about the cost of things." As she says this, thoughts of Lucy and Bas come to mind. The couple, though not married, has been together for years, and while Flannel Lobster only began to experience international attention within the past two or three years, it can't be denied that the lifestyle of her friends *has* changed.

On the other hand, neither Lucy nor Bas squanders money on unnecessary purchases. For the most part, their lives are exactly the same as they were before the band's first single, "Kick It One More Time," took the airwaves by storm: Bas continues to give guitar lessons in his free time while Lucy works her tail off to keep her pottery business afloat. Money hasn't changed them.

But maybe money hasn't changed Max either. He's always had it, after all.

Piper walks over to a table stacked with blue jeans and starts riffling through them. "So did you like him or not?" The question is blunt, though she avoids looking at her cousin as she asks it. "Because he liked *you* a lot. He actually wondered if you'd want to grab dinner again tonight. It's Taco Tuesday at Olé."

"The B.Y.O. Mexican restaurant that you love?"

The accuracy of the statement causes a smile. "Yeah, that's the one."

"I'm up for tacos," Jane assures her. "Can we take margaritas?"

Still grinning, Piper examines a pair of jeans and says, "It's really our only option, isn't it?"

"Sorry to call you at work," Jane says when Marcus answers the phone on the third ring, "but I haven't talked to you since Sunday and I might not get a chance to call later. Piper, Max, and I are going for tacos."

"Ahh, so you're allowing Max a second chance, are you?"

"I didn't hate him or anything. He was just... uppity."

"'Uppity'?" Despite the distance, amusement is evident in Marcus's tone.

"Uppity," Jane repeats. "Like he's better than everyone else."

"How so?"

She groans. "Marcus... I already *told* you about dinner on Sunday! You heard every single one of my observations. Are you seriously going to play devil's advocate now?"

"No, I'm not," he chuckles. "Sorry. I'm sure your instincts are founded." He means it when he says it; there's no hint of sarcasm. "I guess I'm just having a hard time imagining this guy. He doesn't sound like someone who'd make a logical match for Piper."

"That's what I've been saying!" Jane exclaims in exasperation. "I love you, but you're maddening sometimes. Do you realize that?" Without waiting for an answer, she alters the course of the conversation and wonders, "How's Dennis? Is he behaving himself?"

"For the most part, yes. He did chew the corner of the coffee table last night."

"Is it really noticeable?"

"Not very. I take full responsibility for it; I fell asleep on the couch before putting him into his crate."

"Too bad Unc doesn't live on the east coast. He'd be able to fix it in a jiffy." Jane glances at the clock, notices the time. "I should get going. Piper will be here any minute to pick me up. I'll try to give you a call tomorrow, okay?"

"Sure thing, Janie. Have fun tonight. Love you."

"Love you too, Marcus."

ANSEL.

"Let me guess," Ansel says as he watches his daughter and niece squeeze the juice from four halved limes. "Taco Tuesday at Olé?"

"How'd you know?" Piper laughs, giving her father a playful wink.

Ansel knows she will have brought the cointreau and tequila from her own apartment. Not wanting to tempt him, Sophie rarely keeps alcohol of any type in the house... though of course there are exceptions. She'd purchased a bottle of white zinfandel to celebrate Jane's first night with them, and there will be plenty of beer and wine for Friday's rehearsal dinner in the backyard.

He's been sober for three years, two months, and eighteen days.

If it hadn't been for a slip-up when Kai went off to college, the length would be considerably longer. Twenty years or more. Unfortunately, those initial days without kids in the house had been hard for him; Piper had her own apartment by then and Kai was living in the dorms up in Portland. And so Ansel, feeling lonesome, had told his wife he was heading to the public library in search of a distraction.

In actuality, he'd gone to The Library and ordered three rounds of A Midsummer Night's Beam... heavy on the Jim Beam. Despite his size, more than a decade and a half of abstaining from liquor had turned Ansel into a lightweight, but even in his inebriated state, he'd had enough sense to phone Sophie. She'd driven into town, wrapped her arms around him, and folded her husband into the passenger seat of her car. The next day, he'd attended two meetings—one in the morning, the other in the evening—and hasn't had a lapse of judgment since.

His immediate family knows about the setback.

No one else does.

Ansel watches as Piper pulls a shot glass and a bottle of Patrón from the canvas grocery bag she's brought with her. He moves to the refrigerator, pulls a pitcher of blackberry tea from the top shelf, and splashes some of the richly-hued liquid into a glass. Then he carries the sweetened brew to the table and takes a seat, absently scratching at the compass on his wrist. Glancing down, he sees that the needle now hovers to the right, pointing northeast. "Toward the opposite end of town, far away from Olé," he thinks.

And also toward Bend.

Although he can't explain why, Ansel suspects that his ink, this time around, is communicating *through* him... but not *to* him. "Why do I think it's Jane who'd most benefit from the guidance it's providing?" he silently asks himself.

Out loud, he poses, "Are you dead set on those sea bass tacos?"

Piper, in the midst of adding agave syrup to her concoction, looks at her father and narrows her eyes. "I mean, I've only been dreaming about them since I woke up this morning. Why?"

He shrugs. "Just wondering. I know Janie's been there before, is all. I thought you might wanna show her someplace new. Maybe drive into Bend for dinner and see what's going on there."

"I'm up for whatever," Jane assures her cousin. "Mexican's good, but so is pizza. Seriously. I'll eat anything."

Piper crinkles her nose. "We'll be in Bend on Thursday," she says, "for my bachelorette *spa day*." When she speaks the last two words, she lowers her voice, causing the two syllables to sound as though they've just crawled out of a crypt. It's beyond obvious that seaweed wraps and facial massages are *not* something she's looking forward to. "Let's stick with Olé," she decides, capping the syrup. "The margaritas are already made. Is that cool?"

Jane shrugs. "Sure, I'm fine with that."

"I'll show Janie around Bend later in the week," Piper informs her father. "I promise."

JONNY.

Tuesday, 7:25p.m. (PDT)

"Any leads on the frame shop?" Artie asks when he gets home from work. He's dressed in slacks and a button-down, the sleeves rolled up to his elbows and his tie loosened. Jonny knows he does something with sales and insurance, but most of the job description, when he'd been briefed on it yesterday, had gone over his head.

"Nah, not really. I met a guy who suggested I talk to the owner of a sporting goods shop—thought he might know something—but when I drove over there, the store was closed. 'Closed on Tuesdays,' the sign said." He shrugs and takes a sip of the beer he's been working on for the past hour. "I guess I'll try again tomorrow."

Artie notes the can in his friend's hand and arches his brows. "Did you restock my fridge?"

"I sure did."

"Sweet! Best houseguest ever," he deems, and immediately retrieves one of the cold beverages. Then he carries it into the living room and collapses on the couch, tucking his arm beneath his head and studying Jonny. "Are you hungry?"

"A little."

"Wanna try out that flatbread place?"

"Thyme Waits for No One?"

Artie takes a sip of his beer and nods. "I asked one of my coworkers about it today and got directions. It's over near Deschutes. He says it's good. If you don't mind eating out two nights in a row, I thought we could give it a try."

"Yeah, alright," Jonny agrees. "Let's do that."

7:58p.m. (PDT)

Thyme Waits for No One smells decadently of basil, oregano, and garlic. The men grab a table in the middle of the restaurant, claiming the area with a set of car keys before heading up to the counter to place their orders.

There's a line.

A long plank of wood hangs overhead, reminiscent of a cutting board. The menu, divided into three sections, is printed on this in scrolling letters: flatbreads, salads, and sandwiches. As they wait, Jonny considers his options. His mouth waters as he reads the description of a simple margherita pizza.

Three teens manage the counter, ringing up requests and assembling meals. None seems old enough to be in charge and Jonny can't help but wonder if Cory's father is in the back somewhere, silently keeping tabs on his staff.

"Time waits for no one, but I appreciate you waiting for us," the girl working the register says with a smile. "Thanks for being patient. What can I get for you?"

Artie opts for a sub; Jonny sticks with his margherita flatbread.

"We'll bring it out when it's ready," the employee explains, handing each of them a number for their table.

The men fill cups at the soda fountain and carry them back to their seats.

"So," Artie says, "are you still surfing as much as you used to?"

"For the most part, yeah. It helps me clear my head." Jonny's phone vibrates in his pocket, alerting him to a new message. He ignores it and continues, "It's crazy to think that you used to go out with me every morning before class, and now here you are living in a desert."

"In fairness, I lived in a desert *before* college as well," Artie points out, his eyes twinkling. "But I get what you mean. Maybe next summer I'll visit you at the beach. It's been a few years since I've gotten on a board; I wonder if I remember even half of what you taught me."

"Eh, it's like riding a bike. Once you've got it, you've got it for life." He takes a sip of his strawberry Fanta, a guilty pleasure in which he rarely indulges. The soda is bubbly and sweet. "What's your schedule tomorrow?"

"Work all day, dinner with the folks. My mom says she'd love to see you. Will you come?"

It's been years since Jonny's seen Mrs. Beltran. "I'd love to, yeah. What time?"

"Oh... sevenish probably?"

He nods and makes a mental note to be back in Bend by late afternoon. "Sounds good. I'm gonna head into Radio Park tomorrow morning, hopefully catch up with Xavier Kinney—"

"Is that the name of the guy who runs the—"

"Sporting goods shop? Yeah." Jonny shakes his cup, the ice cubes crunching against the waxed-paper container. "And then I guess I'll see where it leads me."

"Alright, well... if you discover the elusive Piper," Artie says, "feel free to bail on dinner. My family and I will completely understand. Although my mom *is* making enmolada..." He grins boyishly and leans back in his chair. "I'm sure you have no idea what that is, but I guarantee you'll like it. Think enchiladas... but better."

Jonny's about to ask what makes them superior, but is interrupted by the delivery of food to their table. Rather than a teenager, the person holding the plates is a woman, and when he looks up, Jonny is pleasantly surprised to find a familiar face. "Natalie!" he exclaims. "I didn't realize you'd be here!"

She laughs and places the flatbread in front of him. "I normally wouldn't be, but my husband had to step out a few hours early today and didn't have anyone older than sixteen to close down the shop. So here I am! I'd normally supervise from afar—I prefer to be hands-off unless the kids need me—but then I saw you and recognized you and wanted to say 'hello.' How's your trip going? Any luck?"

Jonny makes a quick introduction so Artie can be a part of the conversation, then briefs Natalie on his fairly uneventful day. "I'll try again tomorrow," he says, determined to keep his spirits high. "Maybe I'll learn something new."

"You know, when Cory and I got home, I *did* check the backs of my picture frames just to see if the name of the artist or the store was printed there."

"Nothing?"

She offers a dismal shake of her head. "Nothing at all."

"It's alright," Jonny sighs. "I appreciate the attempt. If it's meant to work out, it will."

The words come out sounding confident, but that's not how he feels inside.

Inside, Jonny is beginning to feel both foolish and discouraged.

JANE.

Tuesday, 7:58p.m. (PDT)

Jane plucks another cube of ice from the bucket on the table and drops it into her glass before splashing a bit more margarita on top of it. Her tongue is feeling looser than usual, her cheeks a bit flushed. The tequila is kicking in. She'll need to be extra careful not to spill the beans regarding Thursday; she wishes Bas Porter would call her back.

"Let's talk about the wedding," she decides. "Max, tell me about your groomsmen."

The trio is seated outdoors, their knees practically knocking together under the round wroughtiron table. The remains of sea bass tacos litter their plates, a mostly-empty bowl of guacamole and an equally bare basket of chips cluttering what little free space exists. Maxwell Terrence Storm, III, Esquire provides a charmingly bemused look and reaches over to place a hand on Piper's knee. "Well," he begins, "there are six of them. I believe you're already acquainted with one."

"Yes, Kai shared with me that he'd been recruited. He was a solid choice."

"Thank you. I'm inclined to agree. The others are a bit... older, definitely, and somehow at the same time significantly less mature. Dan and Ryan are senior partners at the firm where I practice—"

"Hardman, Storm, and Storm?" Jane confirms. She knows from listening to Piper brag about her fiance that both Max and his father are name partners. The third fellow, Lester Hardman, was the man who originally opened the firm with the *senior* Maxwell Terrence Storm, Esq. He's since retired, but his name is still on the wall.

"That's right. And then the other guys are friends from law school: Coop Riddlemoser, Jerome Walters, and Cyd Jenkins. Coop and Cyd stuck around the Seattle area; Jerome's living in L.A. He'll fly in late Thursday."

"What about Cyd and Coop?"

Piper leans into Max, turning her face to peer up at him. "They'll be here early Friday, right?"

"That's the plan."

So many people are flying in at the end of the week: Marcus, Jane's mother and father, both brothers and their significant others. Jane is the only member of her family who will be staying with the Fergusons; everyone else has booked hotel rooms in town. Since the wedding is being held on her aunt and uncle's property, this makes for a convenient commute, but it also guarantees that much of her Friday will be consumed by helping Sophie prepare for that evening's rehearsal dinner and the following day's ceremony. She doesn't mind this, of course. Jane is happy to lend a hand.

"Who'll be taking pictures, Pipe? I guess you won't be able to hire the best photographer in town, will you? It'd be hard to capture all the important moments when you're busy experiencing them!"

Piper grins and a subtle flush bleeds through the foundation she's used to cover her asymmetrical freckles. "My friend Siri volunteered. She has an eye for getting just the right shot, so I know she'll do a good job."

"Is she a coworker of yours?"

Jane knows that her cousin recently took a position for a newly-established event planner, Rhoda Trenton-Berg, who moved to Radio Park late last year. Weddings are obviously a popular request, but so are bridal showers, baby showers, and quinceaneras. She imagines more than one photographer is included on the payroll.

"She is," Piper says. "You'll like her a lot. She's quirky, you know?"

Jane doesn't know, but nods nevertheless. She's on a mission to gather a bit of information. "So what's it like being coworkers in the world of photography? Do you work events together, or is it more like a 'meet up in the dark room when it's time to develop film' sort of friendship?"

The comment earns an eye roll from her cousin, but the question *is* meant to be serious.

"I'm honestly curious, Pipe! I mean, I doubt the two of you spend forty hours together each week. It's gotta be different from my job and Max's; we're surrounded by the same people all the time, right?" She glances at the lawyer sitting across from her, waiting for confirmation.

Max relocates the napkin in his lap to his plate, then reaches for his margarita. His slight nod is almost undetectable.

"Siri and I are rarely together for more than eight or nine hours each week," Piper says in response to the query, "but it'll soon be even less than that. I'm going to be switching to part-time after the wedding."

And there it is. What Kai had reported had been factual. Something in Jane's stomach constricts.

JONNY.

Tuesday, 9:43p.m. (PDT)

It isn't until the men have returned to Artie's townhouse and are going about their night-time routines that Jonny fishes his phone from his pocket and first listens to a message from his mother ("Just checking in! Hope you're having fun!"), then reads through the texts from Alex and Owen.

The first comes through in a series of one-sentence messages:

"Miss you, babe.

"I swung by your place this morning and watered the plants, fyi.

"It hasn't rained since you left so things were pretty parched.

"In other news... I met a Komondor last night!!!

"Talk about an unusual breed.

"His name was Swiffer.

"And don't worry: he's fine.

"A ruptured cyst, but the biopsy came back negative.

"OK.

"Love you.

"Miss you.

"Call when you get a chance."

His best friend's communication is much shorter: "Have you found her yet?"

Using his thumbs to type a reply, Jonny responds to Owen first. "Not yet," he writes, "but I've got a lead. Gonna scope it out tomorrow."

Jonny's not in the mood to talk to his mom—or anyone, for that matter—but does send her a short text to let her know that he's fine. He realizes he should do the same for Alex. The problem is, he's just not in the right frame of mind. He has no idea what a Komondor looks like and isn't curious enough to ask Artie if it's alright for him to use his computer to figure it out. He decides to contact her at some point tomorrow. Right now, all he wants is to close his eyes and get a good night's sleep.

Which is exactly what he does.

JANE.

Tuesday, 9:49p.m. (PDT)

They sit in Piper's car with the windows cracked and the faint smoky scent of a bonfire filling the space. The Fergusons' farmhouse looms before them, its vast shape a shadow against the blue-black sky. Sophie has drawn the blinds, but dim squares indicate the interior of the structure is warm and glowing; someone has left the porch light on.

Jane unfastens her seat belt and holds her purse on her lap. She hadn't pursued the topic of her cousin's step back from photography while at the restaurant, but she'd like to now. Taking a deep breath, she wonders, "Why are you giving up on your career? For as long as I've known you, taking pictures has been what you love most. So why give it up?"

"I'm not giving it up," Piper insists. The response is immediate, almost too quick. "I'm just... not allowing it to dictate my life. I don't *need* to work forty hours each week. By taking some time for myself, I'll be able to focus on our house and the life Max and I want to start."

"And what does that entail? Vacuuming every day and making sure dinner's on the table by five?"

"No!"

"Then what? It's not as if you guys have kids yet. There's no reason for you to be a stay-at-home mom... or wife... or *whatever* just yet."

A curtain of dark hair shields Piper's face as she ducks her head. "But we *want* kids."

"Of course you do! That doesn't mean you need to start living like you already have them!"

The radio, barely audible, hums in the background; the quiet notes sound vaguely familiar. When Piper reaches for the knob, increasing the volume, Flannel Lobster's "Uptempo, Down" spills from the speakers: "*Fast is fast and slow is slow; / You need both speeds to make life go. / Reprieves are nice, but so's gusto: / A minute down, then uptempo!*"

"I love this song," Piper sighs, forcing a less-than-convincing smile. "I love the idea of life being a roller coaster and existing at different speeds. Of having fast moments and only knowing they're fast because of the slow moments that put them into perspective." She rests her hands on the steering wheel, leans her head against her seat. "It's not like I've put in my notice yet, Janie. I *could* change my mind."

The fact that she says it is reassuring.

The fact that she apparently hasn't said it to Max isn't.

"He's so particular about so many things," she continues, speaking in a whisper that's hard to hear over the music. Jane wants to silence Sebastian and the boys, but suspects if she does, her cousin will stop communicating. And so she strains her ears and listens.

"He comes from a family that expects things to be perfect, and he's under a lot of pressure to live up to those expectations." She pauses and chews her lip for a moment before continuing, "His parents wanted to have the rehearsal dinner at this really fancy restaurant in town, but that didn't make sense to me. We're getting married at my *parents' house*, so the rehearsal dinner should be *at my parents' house*. Don't you agree?"

Jane nods.

"It took Max forever to persuade his mom, Gloria, that it made more sense to do something low-key. But low-key for the Storms is still a big production. They're having crabs shipped overnight from *Maryland*. Do you have any idea how *expensive* that is?" She rolls her eyes. "I would've been fine with hamburgers and hotdogs."

Jane has only known Max for a handful of hours and he's still very much a stranger to her. Nevertheless, she can't imagine him at a backyard picnic. The gathering seems entirely too casual.

As the last notes of "Uptempo, Down" filter from the speakers, Piper turns to her cousin and insists, "He's a good man, Janie—honestly, he is—and I really want you to like him. I want you to be able to see him the way I do. To look past his expensive clothes and big-time job and see him for who he is on the inside. Max is sweet, and kind, and he loves me for me."

Wednesday, 12:13a.m. (PDT)

"Max doesn't love her for her," Kai all but spits when Jane shares this line a few hours later. "He's got her brainwashed into *thinking* he loves her for her." He pulls a can of seltzer from the refrigerator and cracks it open, the sound that it makes a soft *pfft!*

Jane perches on the counter, sipping a mug of peppermint tea, and watches her cousin. He's still dressed in his work clothes: khakis and a Terrible Terrier Brewing t-shirt. His hair is disheveled and his youthful cheeks boast a light dusting of whiskers that, on a man older than he, might be described as a five o'clock shadow. As it is, it's taken Kai until well past midnight to acquire such a scruff. "I wish she'd break up with him," he grumbles in a way that a disgruntled teenager might. "I can't stand him."

"Believe it or not, I've picked up on this."

Grinning despite himself, Kai slurps his seltzer and asks, "Do you remember that time Piper flew east to see you and got stuck in Colorado on the way home and met that guy in a shady bar and they talked until tomorrow?" The words come out in a run-on; zero punctuation is employed until the question mark at the end. "She was completely smitten for, like, two months after that. I can remember wishing she'd track him down and get together with him. The way she talked about him made him seem like a genuinely good guy."

Jane bites her bottom lip and waltzes backwards through her memories, trying to recall a story about being stranded in Colorado that involved a potential love interest for her cousin. And yet, no matter how hard she focuses, nothing comes to mind. "How long ago was that?"

"I don't know. Five or six years? When was the last time Piper visited you in Pennsylvania?"

"Um... Probably five or six years ago."

"Yeah. So I was right." Kai grins. "The guy was a surfer. I remember that because I thought it was really cool at the time. Admittedly, I still think it's pretty cool, but it seemed *extra* cool when I was only fifteen years old."

Jane laughs, but she doesn't disagree. Just the idea of a surfer—someone in tune with nature and willing to take risks—better complements her cousin's personality than a man like Maxwell Terrence Storm, III, Esq. "Do you remember anything else about him?" she wonders now. "His name, maybe? Or where he was from?"

Kai thinks for a moment, pulling back the tab of his can and releasing it so it makes a metallic *click* each time it connects with the lid. His mind is void of additional details, though, and he eventually shakes his head to indicate such. With one corner of his mouth slanting upwards, he says, "But *that's* the kind of guy I always imagined for my sister—not some high-and-mighty lawyer who wears three-hundred-dollar ties and doesn't own a single article of clothing that doesn't need to be dry cleaned."

JONNY.

Wednesday, 8:08a.m. (PDT)

Having wasted a good chunk of yesterday morning in bed, Jonny makes it a point to rise early. He starts his day with a short-but-brisk run through Artie's neighborhood, hops into the shower right afterward, and is driving past the little sign welcoming him to Radio Park only minutes after eight o'clock. It isn't until he's actually found his way back to Hike-Camp-Repeat and is reaching for the handle of the plate-glass door that he reads the hours posted there in the window:

Monday: 10am-6pm

Tuesday: CLOSED

Wednesday: 10am-6pm

Thursday: 10am-6pm

Friday: 9am-6pm

Saturday: 9am-6pm

Sunday: 10am-5pm

"Well, shit," he mutters, running a hand over his buzzed hair. "Now what?"

Having scarfed a bowl of cereal before leaving Bend, he isn't exactly hungry, but a strong cup of coffee sounds really good right about now.

Jonny leaves his car where it's parked and sets off down the sidewalk, navigating the quiet side streets in search of a busier section of town.

Already, the day is warm. While eating his granola, he'd scanned the newspaper Artie had abandoned on the kitchen table, checking the weather and learning the highs would be well into the nineties today. On the plus side, a lack of humidity makes the dry heat surprisingly bearable—so much so that he may not necessarily feel compelled to order an iced beverage.

At the Bender Boulevard intersection, Jonny looks left, then right, squinting against the sun. "Cup o' Mud Buzz," he mutters aloud, catching sight of the circular sign out front. "Now *that* sounds like coffee." He quickens his pace, suddenly eager to consume some much-needed caffeine.

While the outside of the coffeehouse boasts colors best described by the drinks the venue is known for, the inside is bright and colorful. A pattern of paisley papers one of the walls; the tables and chairs are suggestive of citrus. Things like clementines, tangelos, and mandarin oranges come to mind. There's a purple couch too, upholstered in corduroy and adorned with yellow pillows. They match the sunshiny door through which Jonny had entered.

The air is heavy with the nutty aroma of coffee. The soundtrack of the shop is a medley of frothing and grinding and modern music. Jonny instantly recognizes the melody blasting from ceiling-mounted speakers, and when he starts to whistle along, a shaggy-haired man preparing a latte at the back of the store looks up and grumbles, "Can I just say that I am so sick of this song? And this band. They're everywhere, all the time. They're even here tomorrow."

"Here?"

"In Radio Park, on the other side of town at the Post Press. It's a sold-out show, of course."

The animosity the barista exudes in regards to Flannel Lobster is almost palpable. Jonny quirks an eyebrow and tilts his head. "Sounds like you're not exactly their number-one fan."

"Ha! No, not by a long shot." He places a plastic lid on the drink he's been making and walks out from behind the counter, delivering the beverage to a young woman sitting nearby. A dog lounges at her feet and Jonny recognizes it as a blue merle Australian Shepherd. As the visitor approaches, the pup's ears go up and his back end begins to wiggle.

"Vanilla latte with extra espresso," the barista says, setting the cup on the table and fishing a biscuit from his pocket. He bends down to offer it to the dog. To the person, he adds, "Let me know if you need a refill, Mary." Then, turning his attention back to Jonny, he apologizes, "Your first impression of me is probably that I'm a giant curmudgeon. Sorry about that."

"Hey, not a problem. We can't all like the same music, right?"

"A valid point." The tall man smiles and slips back behind the bar. "I'm Chet, by the way. One of the owners. Is this your first time here?"

"It's my first time in Radio Park, actually."

"Oh, yeah? Are you here on vacation?"

"Uh... sort of?" Jonny studies the chalkboard menu hanging above him, skimming his options. "I guess my secondary reason for being here is vacation, but my primary reason's a bit more complicated. I'm looking for a girl."

Chet lifts his honey-golden brows, intrigued. "Will just any girl do, or are you looking for one in particular? Because my sister Lara's available and she'd be a real catch."

Jonny can feel his cheeks growing rosier by the second. Laughing a bit awkwardly, he admits, "I met her six years ago and pretty much all I know about her is that her name's Piper, she's from Radio Park, and her dad, who *possibly* owned a framing shop, has a bunch of tattoos. Does any of that sound familiar?"

"Nope."

"Yeah, I wasn't really expecting it to."

"The thing is, I haven't been in Radio Park all that long either," Chet offers. "I only moved here about five months ago. Before that, I was in California—that's where I grew up—and before *that*, I was actually living in Pennsylvania. My brother and I ran a coffee shop there; Joe still does."

"What brought you back out west?"

Chet rolls his eyes toward the ceiling, glaring at the nearest speaker as the last few bars of "Uptempo, Down" pour out of it. "This band, believe it or not. The lead singer essentially stole my girlfriend." His tone, when he says it, is flat and riddled with annoyance.

Jonny hadn't been expecting an answer quite like the one that's been volunteered. He widens his eyes, amazed. "Gosh... That explains a lot. No wonder Flannel Lobster isn't your favorite band. I get it now."

Attempting to move away from memories of the unfortunate situation, Chet lifts his shoulders in a shrug and rests his hand on a stack of cups. "It is what it is, right? I mean, there's not much I can do about it now."

"True."

"So what'll you have?"

Craving something on the sweeter side, Jonny opts for a large mochaccino.

"Whipped cream on top?" Chet confirms.

"Why not?"

9:36a.m. (PDT)

He spends an hour at Cup o' Mud Buzz, passing the time by chatting with Chet and perusing the pages of a Radio Park publication the barista provides. The informative magazine mirrors the title of the town, offering page-long stories about local business owners and new attractions. Jonny skims an article about a restaurant called On the Side, intrigued by the concept of specializing in side dishes rather than entrees, and is about to read an interview called "Getting to Know... Rhoda Trenton-Berg, Radio Park's newest event planner" when he notes the time. He makes it through the first paragraph, learning the name of the company (Put THAT on the Calendar!) and its early history (it opened about six months ago, in early February), but closes the magazine and sets it aside before being introduced to Rhoda's all-female staff.

Getting to his feet, Jonny rests the publication on the middle couch cushion and turns to the lanky canine he'd been sharing the space with: a whippet by the name of Annabel. Upon her arrival, she had refused to join her human and Italian Greyhound sister at one of the nearby tables. "She's a primadonna, that one," the man holding the other end of her leash had said when Annabel first wandered over. "Don't want nothin' to do with the dog beds I buy her 'cos she thinks she belongs on the couch." He'd rolled his eyes and followed up with, "Do you mind if she sits beside you?"

Jonny hadn't.

Now he gives Annabel a final scratch behind her ears and raises his hand in farewell. "Thanks again for the coffee," he calls back to Chet, "and good luck with the shop!"

"Hey, I appreciate it. If you need another caffeine fix while you're in town, feel free to stop by."

ANSEL.

Ansel is in the midst of framing a unique series of artwork—four olives, one conductor and three playing instruments, each mounted on a six-by-six-inch canvas—when his niece appears in his studio. Her hair is damp, still dripping from the shower, and her cheeks are flushed. She carries with her the scent of rosemary. "Unc!" she exclaims, her tone breathless and animated. "I just talked to Bas!"

Glancing up from the mat he'd been about to cut, Ansel arches his brows. Assuming "Bas" is the name of someone, he has no idea who she's talking about. "Am I meant to know who that person is?" he wonders.

Jane takes a deep breath and walks over to stand before him. Her eyes are wild. She leans against the worktable in front of her, fixing her gaze on his. "Bas Porter is the lead singer of Flannel Lobster," she explains. Her voice is deceptively calm. "Flannel Lobster will be in Radio Park tomorrow. They're playing at that venue we passed yesterday in town—"

"The Post Press?"

She nods. "I know it's sold out, but one of my best friends is *dating* Bas. He's from Lake Caywood, you know? Where I went to college? Anyway..." Jittery with anticipation, it's obvious that Jane is struggling to organize her

128

thoughts. "Anyway," she repeats, "Bas just called and the band will be in town early tomorrow morning, and he's not only hooking me up with eight tickets to the show, but he's *also* wondering if we have any interest in spending the day with him and the band. I said 'yes!' Piper is going to be *floored!*"

It's a lot of information to take in, and as Ansel slowly processes through it, several questions formulate in his mind. Completely abandoning the olive marching band spread before him, he runs a calloused hand over his bald head and proceeds to gather a few more details. "First of all, I feel it necessary to state the obvious: tomorrow is the bachelorette party. Now, while I do remember you mentioning how you'd like to switch things up, I guess I didn't realize you'd actually taken the steps to do so. This is all pretty last-minute, Janie-girl."

"Right, I know... but isn't the plan so much better now? Goodbye, spa day; *hellooo*, dancing and margaritas! With *Flannel Lobster*, Unc. These guys are a big freakin' deal right now. That song Aunt Sophie likes so much? 'Uptempo, Down'? It was the number-one song in the *country* last week. And we have the opportunity to go *tubing* with them tomorrow afternoon. You can't tell me not to carpe diem the *shit* out of this opportunity; I'd be a fool not to take advantage of it."

There isn't a doubt in Ansel's mind that his daughter will prefer the new arrangement, but he also can't deny the reservations he's feeling in regards to the anticipated reaction from Marta Storm. The woman is someone who tends to get what she wants. So much so, in fact, that when she married her husband—Dr. Nathan Baxter—she'd been so adamant about keeping her last name that she'd actually required *him* to drop "Baxter" and take "Storm." Piper had rolled her eyes while sharing the story, adding, "I think it probably had a lot to do with all the monogrammed paraphernalia she has. I've never met anyone with so much monogrammed *shit*."

At the time, the anecdote had been humorous, but then Ansel had gotten to know Marta a bit better and had seen her true colors. As Susannah Lerner, captain of the mighty fishing vessel known as the *Harvey John*, would have said, "She's a real piece of work, that one. Got her knickers in a twist and her panties in a wad." The expression had always seemed a bit redundant to Ansel, but when applied to Max's older sister, the redundancy merely reinforces the truth.

"I suppose my concern," he confides to his niece, "is that Marta may in fact kill you."

"My concern," Jane counters, "is that I told Bas I'd take care of gathering all the supplies needed for a day on the river. If there are four of them and eight of us—"

"Eight?"

"Kai's coming," she says dismissively. "He's been in on this since the get-go."

"Ahh," Ansel sighs, unsurprised by the admission. He can remember a time many, many years ago when, while visiting Cape Cod, he and his sister's families had been forced to endure a dinner of potato salad, corn-on-the-cob, and little else after learning that the main course had been released into the wild by his son and niece.

"We're going to need twelve tubes, one of those inflatable kiddie pools to hold all the beer, and a whole bunch of ice. I looked at the weather; tomorrow's supposed to be even hotter than today."

"And just when are you planning to break the news to Marta?"

For the first time since appearing in his studio, Jane looks a little uncertain. "So... about that," she mumbles. "Kai's going to reach out to Maude, and Maude's going to *hopefully* explain the situation to her sister, call the spa to cancel the reservation, and arrange for everyone to meet here at eleven o'clock tomorrow morning."

The location throws Ansel for a loop.

His face must convey his confusion because Jane says, "Bas offered to pick us up. In their tour bus! I couldn't say no to that." She grins mischievously. "Kai and I aren't gonna breathe a word of it to Piper until tomorrow morning. I hope she doesn't faint or something."

Imagining the expression on his daughter's face when she sees a tour bus pull up in front of the barn is enough to make Ansel laugh out loud. "I need to hand it to you, Janie-girl: you seem to have pulled it off. I guess you and Kai'll be lightheaded by this evening, huh? You've got an awful lot of tubes to blow up."

"Oh! That's actually why I'm here," Jane says brightly. "Kai had to switch some things around at work so he can be off tomorrow. He goes in at noon today and won't be home 'til late. Can you give me a ride into town so I can stock up on rafts and things?"

Her eyes are so twinkly that Ansel can't in good conscience refuse.

JONNY.

Wednesday, 10:18a.m. (PDT)

"Xavier won't be in until twelve o'clock," the sales associate informs Jonny. "I can either have him call you, or you can stop back then. Whichever works better for you."

A massive exhale exits his lungs as yet another wave of defeat washes over him. "Yeah, alright. I'll come back a little bit later. Thanks." With slumped shoulders and his head hanging, Jonny turns his back on the sporting goods store and steps back into the desert heat of Radio Park. He checks his watch, ponders how he might be able to productively pass the next two hours, and meanders down Water Street. The soles of his shoes scuff the sidewalk as he drags his feet over the hot cement, propelling himself toward the river.

He finds a bench that looks out on the water, claims a section of it shaded by a tall Ponderosa pine. Several yards away, a trio of teenagers wades along the bank, bare chested and carrying fishing poles. They cast their lines as far out as they can manage, the red-and-white bobbers all but a speck in the glistening waves.

A good half mile out, various groups of tubers head south; passing them in the opposite direction, a kayaker works her way upstream. The sight reminds him of something Piper had said that night at the bar so long ago: "I think it would be so neat to say that I've swum the English Channel."

"Is that something you'd like to do at some point?"

"Not really, no. I'm not an especially good swimmer."

Jonny remembers lifting an eyebrow and feeling utterly perplexed. "But you *can* swim, right?"

"Of course I can swim!" Piper had laughed, and then swatted him lightly on the bicep. "I'm no Amy Van Dyken, but I do alright."

"Amy who?"

"Amy Van Dyken. She won, like, all of the gold medals at the last Olympic Games."

"All of 'em, huh?"

"Well, maybe not all of them... but I think she got four or five."

The two had fallen silent after that, sipping their drinks and thinking their own private thoughts. Jonny's mind had traveled first to Atlanta, recalling how even his small hometown of Moonglow, North Carolina, had benefited from the Games occurring several hundreds of miles away, and then to the English Channel as he'd attempted to remember the name of the first woman who swam it. It had taken a while to come up with the information, but when the words "Gertrude Ederle" finally popped into his head, he'd wasted zero time in speaking them aloud.

"Hmm?" Piper had wondered dreamily, and so Jonny had repeated, a bit more confidently this time, "Gertrude Ederle. She swam the English Channel in the nineteen-twenties, I think. I read a biography about her a few years ago; she's an interesting person."

"Is she still alive?"

"I'm not sure," he'd admitted. "If she is, she's gotta be close to a hundred. Maybe even older."

Now, sitting on a bench in Radio Park and watching the action taking place on the river before him, he thinks back on that conversation and wonders if Piper has improved her stroke.

He wonders if she *still* thinks it would be neat to say she's swum the English Channel, or if she's moved onto goals that are better suited to her skillset.

Most of all, he wonders if he might eventually be able to stand right in front of her and simply ask all of the questions that continue to bounce off the walls of his skull. With each passing day, they seem to multiply.

"Where are you, Piper?" he whispers now. "Where are you hiding?"

11:44a.m. (PDT)

Knowing he can't put it off forever, Jonny calls Alex before heading back to Hike-Camp-Repeat.

She sounds groggy when she answers and it occurs to him that she might have been sleeping. It's almost three o'clock on the east coast, but a week of night shifts always wreaks havoc on her schedule. "Did I wake you?" he asks. "I'm sorry."

"No, it's fine."

Jonny can hear the smile in her voice. He imagines her mussed hair and the way she'll undoubtedly use the middle finger of her right hand to pick at the kernels of sleep that cling to the corners of her eyes.

"I need to get up soon anyway. How're you? How's Oregon?"

"It's good, yeah. Hot."

"Have you done much hiking?"

"Uh... not really. Not yet, anyway. I'm hoping to get into some of that tomorrow or the next day." The statement is a blatant lie. If he weren't completely preoccupied by his ludicrous mission, he'd be spending every day exploring the Cascade Mountains, but as it is, time is quickly slipping away from him. Wanting to change the topic, he prompts, "So, hey. What's a Komondor? Did I get the pronunciation right? I assume it's a breed of dog."

"You did!" Alex praises. "And yes, it is. They're big—like, over a hundred pounds—and their fur is corded."

"Wait. What d'you mean?"

"They've got dreadlocks."

"Oh."

"And they're white. They look like big mops."

The name Swiffer suddenly makes a bit of sense. "Oh," Jonny repeats, this time drawing out the word in a way that suggests it ought to be spelled with more than just two letters. "Huh."

"Yeah."

"Yeah."

The silence that ensues feels awkward to Jonny; he wonders if Alex is having a similar thought.

"So," he eventually says, wanting to fill the dead air with something more than the sound of his girlfriend's quiet breathing, "I should probably get going. I just wanted to touch base and let you know I got your message."

"I'm glad you called. It's good to hear your voice."

"Yeah, yours too."

"I love you, Jonny."

"Yep. I love you too. I'll give you a call in a couple days, alright?"

"Alright," she agrees, sounding maybe, *just maybe*, a smidge insecure. "Bye, Jonny."

"Bye, Alex."

The feeling he experiences when he ends the call is equal parts guilt and relief. Rather than dwell on this complicated combination, however, he gets to his feet and heads back in the direction of the sporting goods store. With any luck, Xavier Kinney will be available for a quick conversation.

JANE.

"You don't want to come in with me?" Jane asks when her uncle doesn't make any move to exit his vehicle. She stands on the sidewalk in front of Hike-Camp-Repeat, her hand on the open passenger door as she addresses Ansel, still seated in the cab.

"I do not," he says, "but I'll be back in about thirty minutes to pick you up. Your aunt asked me to swing by the florist and pay the remainder of our balance. I'm going to do that while you stockpile tubes, unless you tell me otherwise."

Jane smiles and shakes her head. "Nah, I've got this. Twelve innertubes, one kiddie pool, and we'll stop for ice on the way home?"

"Correct." Ansel crinkles his forehead, running through the list of supplies. "At what point are you buying the alcohol?" he asks curiously. "I understand why you may not want to request that we do it today, but I'm fully capable of walking into a grocery store and helping you transport a few cases of beer to the car. That's not going to make me want a drink, Janie-girl. Honest."

"I appreciate that, but Kai volunteered to bring an assortment of stuff from the Terrible Terrier. I guess he gets an employee discount or something?" She shrugs and glances toward the sporting goods store behind her, eager to get inside. The prospect of tomorrow is exciting; she's been feeling as though her blood is sizzling with electricity ever since she got off the phone with Bas. "Thirty minutes," she confirms with her uncle. "I'll meet you out front."

The door to the pickup makes a muted *thwump* as it swings shut.

12:01p.m. (PDT)

Although it doesn't appear especially large from the outside, Hike-Camp-Repeat is deceivingly vast. The building itself is deep, the shelving units and display racks inside packed tightly with all sorts of outdoorsy equipment. It takes Jane a few moments to determine the layout of the store, realizing that land accoutrements are housed near the front while anything pertaining to the water can be found in the back. She passes by a collection of fishing rods and tackle boxes, weaves her way through several racks of life vests and wetsuits, and eventually stumbles upon a back wall lined with shelves housing everything from slip-and-slides to squirt guns, diving rings to snorkels.

Because floating is a popular pastime during the summer months, the selection of inner tubes is expansive. Jane opts for a middle-of-the-road model, loading up her cart with thirteen of them just in case one develops a hole. She has a fun time mixing and matching the colors, buying a few in every shade: green, yellow, and red. "Like a traffic light," she muses to herself, then meanders down the aisle in search of inflatable pools.

Kai has promised a minimum of three cases, insisting he'd rather provide too much beer than too little. "Just make sure that whichever pool you buy will hold *all* of the booze," he'd said before leaving the house earlier this morning. "And get at least three bags of ice. The big bags. Ten pounds, not five. Okay?"

"You sure are bossy," she'd teased, but promised to follow the instructions to a T.

It's as she's debating between a clear pool or, for two dollars more, one that's printed to resemble the inside of a watermelon, that she spies an attractive customer talking to one of the sales associates. He's on the taller side, though not overly so, and his hair is a sandy shade of brown. He wears it short, the stuff on his head not all that much longer than the scruff on his face. "Cute," Jane decides, and sneaks a second, longer look as he speaks quietly to the employee.

The man's fashion sense is laid back and fun: white t-shirt, dark khakis rolled a few inches above his ankles, canvas boat shoes the color of weathered ash. He looks to be about the same age as Jane. Apparently sensing her stare, he glances in her direction, offering a shy smile that seems to come from his eyes rather than his mouth.

"Sure, let me get him," the associate says in response to whatever the man has requested. She's grinning as she turns and disappears into the back room.

Jane resumes her task of selecting a swimming pool, opting for the fruitier version and placing it in her cart. Then she wheels her way toward the front of the store.

"Looks like you and quite a few of your friends are planning to spend some time on the water," the man with the kind eyes says as she passes. His voice has a comforting southern drawl to it.

"I'm prepping for a last-minute switcheroo to my cousin's bachelorette party. We were supposed to go to the spa, but that's just not her style. Instead, we're gonna spend tomorrow on the river and then follow it up with a concert."

"Flannel Lobster?"

Jane beams. "How'd you know?"

"Eh, I heard they were gonna be in town. Have fun!"

"Thanks! We will." As she walks away, Jane can't help but think she'd be all about flirting with such a handsome fellow if she weren't already involved with Marcus. He is one fine-looking specimen...

JONNY.

Wednesday, 12:14p.m. (PDT)

Jonny watches the girl with the strawberry-blonde locks as she heads toward the register. The bachelorette party she's in the midst of organizing sounds like a fun time and he realizes if he *does* decide to propose to Alex, Owen could easily plan a similar outing for his bachelor party. Moonglow may not have a river, but it has an ocean; the men could tube behind a boat and it would be equally enjoyable.

Lost in thoughts of festivities surrounding a wedding that may never happen, he doesn't immediately hear the office door behind him swing open. It isn't until a spry, elderly gentleman stands before him, the buttons of his shirt misaligned and one of his hiking boots untied. His wavy grey hair is slicked back and his thick spectacles are smudged with fingerprints. Jonny wonders how he can see out of them. "Hi there!" Xavier Kinney says as he extends a hand for shaking. His skin is leathery, as if he's spent a good chunk of his life in the sun. "I hear you've got a few questions I might be able to answer."

"I do, yeah. I'm attempting to track down the owner of a frame shop that closed a few years ago. Unfortunately, the only information I have to go on is a vague location—Radio Park—and the possibility that the owner had a lot of tattoos. Does that ring any bells?"

"Sure does," Xavier answers immediately. "The shop was called You've Been Framed and the marketing was real clever-like. One whole wall—the one right there in the front, soon as you walked in—was covered in nothin' but mugshots. Famous ones. Frank Sinatra, Elvis Presley... Dr. Martin Luther King, Jr." He pauses, scratches his head. "David Bowie, I think, and some of the real bad guys like Al Capone and John Dillinger, too. Each one had its own style of frame: wood, metal... matted, without. It was an interestin' way to showcase a person's options, you see. But like you said, the owner closed up shop a few years back."

The information is more than Jonny had been hoping to receive; he's begun to grow accustomed to disappointment. "You don't by any chance remember the name of the man who ran it, do you?" It's with bated breath that he waits, the fingers of his right hand crossing instinctively.

"I'm sorry to say that I don't. He was a nice man—I spoke to him once or twice—but I'm not sure I'd recognize his name even if I tripped over it. It could be that I can put you in touch with someone who has that information, though. My friend Alice Clodham is more attuned to the art world than I. If you give me a minute, I'll get her number for you."

1:17p.m. (PDT)

The number Xavier Kinney provides goes straight to voicemail every time Jonny dials it and the robotic voice that informs him of this also lets him know that the mailbox is full... which is why he stops at the public library and uses one of the available computers to search the name "Alice Clodham."

There are apparently three A. Clodhams living in Radio Park.

He writes down the address for each one, then closes the browser and approaches a librarian about perusing old newspaper articles. "I'm looking for anything that might put me in touch with an artist named Alice Clodham," he explains.

"This is an easy one!" the librarian laughs. She's on the younger side and wears her long hair in a sloppy bun on the top of her head. "Alice is one of our local artists. Watercolors, mostly. She sells her paintings in a tiny gallery on Third Street, but she can usually be found down by the water in Ponderosa Park. She might be there now, although you'd have a better shot of catching up with her first thing in the morning; I know the light's better then."

"Ponderosa Park?" Jonny repeats, pulling a folded sheet of paper from his pocket and jotting this down underneath the addresses. "Is that nearby?"

The librarian scrunches her nose, bringing it closer to her eyes. "Not too far," she reasons. "Maybe a fifteen-minute drive? I can give you directions if that would help. It's certainly not difficult to find."

"That would be great," Jonny thanks her. "That would be really, really helpful."

Ponderosa Park is far from empty when he arrives, but the only person with an easel and palette of paint is a man who looks to be at least eighty years old. An elderly dachshund sits at his feet, his copper-hued snout peppered with white.

"You don't by any chance know of a woman named Alice Clodham, do you?" Jonny wonders, approaching the artist from behind. The canvas he's working on is a large one, the image he's painting reminiscent of something Bob Ross might create. Both the clouds and the pine trees appear happy.

The man's voice, when he answers, is as creaky as an old door. "Alice'll be back early tomorrow," he says without looking up from his masterpiece. "I expect she'll show up around half-past six." He coughs, gathers phlegm in his mouth, spits it into the shaggy grass and adds, "Usually does."

"Half-past six," Jonny mutters to himself. "Huh. Okay. Wow. That's really early."

ANSEL.

Wednesday, 8:45p.m. (PDT)

Sophie stands behind her husband, traipsing her fingers over his neck as he sits at the family's computer and browses Flannel Lobster's webpage. "I just don't know that I've seen such a handsome group of musicians since Ed Sullivan hosted The Beatles," she sighs, bending down and placing her cheek against Ansel's. She's just returned from the bath and smells pleasantly of powder. "Look at them, honey... They're all so pretty!"

Ansel rolls his eyes and guides his cursor to the next picture, clicking on it to enlarge the image. Four men, all around the same age as Piper and Jane. They stand with their arms around each other, two with dark hair, one almost blonde, and the fourth sporting a wild array of dreadlocks. "Pretty" is not a word he would use to describe any of them; "artsy," on the other hand, is.

"Piper isn't going to know how to react tomorrow. I hope Janie's prepared to catch her if she passes out."

"I think she's prepared for that outcome; she made a similar comment earlier this morning."

Sophie giggles into his ear. The sound creates a gentle tickle. "Are she and Kai upstairs finalizing the details right now? I thought I heard him come home while I was in the tub."

"He's here, yes, but I think they're stocking the basement refrigerator at the moment. I could be wrong." Ansel gives his wife's hand an affectionate squeeze before vacating his seat. "I'll leave this browser open for you. Feel free to continue swooning over these boys who are young enough to be your sons." His voice is teasing, his manner kind. He brushes his fingers over the small of her back as he walks away. "I think I'll head upstairs. Join me whenever you're ready."

9:03p.m. (PDT)

Standing in front of the bathroom mirror, Ansel runs his left thumb over the compass tattooed on his right wrist. Its needle has been spinning at a nearly imperceptible speed all afternoon. The motion pulls at his skin, tugging just enough to create a level of discomfort, but not enough to cause pain.

He feels antsy. Unsettled. He can recall only one instance redolent of this one, and it had occurred right after Kai left for college. Back then, too much Jim Beam and a momentary lapse of control is what had transpired, but something in *this* experience feels different. There's beer in the house—Ansel is well aware of this—but he doesn't have the urge to drink. His thoughts, instead, are on his tattoo.

When had the needle begun its roundabout route? Was it before or after his niece briefed him on the change of plans regarding Piper's bachelorette party?

He can't remember.

He wishes he could.

He wonders if it might have begun shortly following his trip into town.

He wonders, too late, if he'd been meant to set foot inside Hike-Camp-Repeat.

JONNY.

Wednesday, 9:34p.m. (PDT)

"Dinner was excellent, Mrs. Beltran. Thank you so much for having me." Jonny bends down, wrapping the slight woman in his arms, and then straightens up to offer his hand to Artie's father. "It was good seeing you again, sir. I appreciate the hospitality."

"You are welcome here any time, Jonathan," Mrs. Beltran says, taking his hand in hers as she does. She is one of the only people on the planet who refuses to call him by his nickname. In the same vein, she always refers to her son as "Arturo" rather than "Artie."

"If it didn't require a full day of travel, I'd take you up on that offer at least once a week," he assures her. "Everything was delicious. Really."

"Next time you come to Bend, you look us up," Mr. Beltran says good-naturedly. He rests a hand on his little potbelly and turns to his wife. "I go to bed now, *mi amada*." And without further ado, the man turns and heads upstairs.

"And... that's a wrap," Artie says, shaking his head in amusement. "Papa is nothing if not direct. I'll give you a call this weekend, Ma." He plants a kiss on her cheek, then claps a hand on Jonny's shoulder. "I need to get this guy home; he's got an early morning."

The ride back to the townhouse is relatively tranquil. Artie fiddles with the radio, tuning it to a station that plays hits from the eighties on Wednesday nights and tapping his thumbs against the steering wheel as Dexy's Midnight Runners sings about a love that's not yet jaded or beaten down.

Jonny drowses in the seat beside him, pondering the lyrics and wondering why he's never really pondered them before.

"What're you thinking about over there?" Artie prompts after a while. "Are you still awake?"

Yawning himself into a more upright position, Jonny opens his eyes and says, "D'you remember how, back when we were in college, Bruiser used to talk about things from the past? Anytime anyone brought something up from long ago, he'd point at 'em and say, 'Now *that's* taking a trip in the Wayback Machine!'"

"Sure, I remember!" Artie laughs. "It's a reference to *Rocky and Bullwinkle*, isn't it?"

"I mean, I guess so? I just always associate it with Bruiser."

"Yeah, I suppose I do too." He glances briefly at his passenger, turns the radio down a smidge. "What made you think of that? Are you feeling nostalgic or something?"

Jonny forces a chuckle even though he doesn't feel especially funny at the moment. "Maybe a little bit. Imagine you had access to the Wayback Machine, though. Would you take a ride in it? Where would you go?"

"I know where *you'd* go," Artie muses. "Denver, Colorado, circa six years ago. And you'd ask Piper for her last name."

"And her phone number, and her mailing address, and her social security number," Jonny jokes.

"Ha! I'll bet. And then she would've tossed her drink in your face and booked it back to the airport, where she'd promptly board a flight to absolutely anywhere in order to ensure she was putting as much distance as possible between herself and her newfound stalker."

Jonny laughs, this time for real. "Yeah, I guess you're right. A social security number would be a bit over the top."

"Oh, you think?"

He's quiet for several moments as he hypothesizes about the impossible scenario. It isn't until Artie pulls into his driveway and shuts off the car's engine that Jonny speaks again, and then it is only to say, "If I had it to do over again, I would definitely ask for her number."

Thursday, 6:08a.m. (PDT)

Whereas Cup o' Mud Buzz had been experiencing a steady flow of foot traffic when Jonny was in yesterday, the establishment is quiet this morning. He runs a hand over his scraggly cheeks as he pushes through the bright yellow door. Normally clean shaven, he hasn't picked up his razor since arriving in Oregon; he's not used to the scruff on his face.

"You're back!" Chet greets him, and the warmth in his voice suggests that he's actually quite glad to see him. "And you look as though you might benefit from an extra shot of espresso in whatever it is you're drinking today. What'll it be?" He leans the broom he'd been using against the counter and moves to the other side of the bar. "Another mochaccino?"

"Actually, I'm gonna go with an incredibly strong Americana today."

The barista lifts his brows. "Should I leave room for cream?"

"Nah," Jonny says with a shake of his head. "Go ahead and fill it to the brim."

Laughing, Chet sets to work, and as he prepares the beans that he'll use for the beverage, he raises his voice to be heard over the grinder. "Seeing as you're back in Radio Park at the crack of dawn, I presume you haven't found her yet."

It's a statement rather than a question.

Jonny nods glumly to substantiate the assumption. "I do have a lead, though. There's an artist who sets up camp each morning at Ponderosa Park—Alice Clodham's her name—and there's a *chance* she might know the name of the guy who owned and operated You've Been Framed."

"You've Been Framed?" Chet confirms, cracking a smile. "That's the name of the frame shop?"

"It was, yeah. Pretty funny, huh?"

He answers with a bemused snort, then says, "So you're off to make the acquaintance of Alice Clodham. She's a bit of a free spirit, you know. You might wanna brace yourself for that."

"Oh, yeah?"

"Oh, yeah. You're in for a real experience."

"The man you're asking about is named Ansel Ferguson and he's one of the finest woodworkers in the state. Now don't get me wrong: Ansel did a nice job of framing—and still does, as far as I know—but the man makes the nicest chairs you've ever sat on before. Rocking chairs, Adirondack chairs, regular old kitchen chairs," Alice says with a theatrical flap of her hands. "Ansel has... Now how do I say this? A knack? A gift? These nouns, they're not *exact* enough to explain what I mean." And then settling on the proper terminology, "Ansel Ferguson has a fluid *grace* about him when it comes to working with wood. He's a master."

Jonny opens his mouth to ask about where he might find Ansel Ferguson, but is unable to form even a single syllable before Alice waves her paintbrush in front of his face and continues, "His wife Sophie, she's an artist as well. Now and again she'll hang a piece of artwork at the same gallery where I hang mine. Have you been in? It's called Third Street Gallery and it's conveniently located on Third Street. If you have some free time, you should really pay it a visit. The girl who runs the facility is such a sweetheart. Jody's, her name, with a Y on the end. Built like a willow, that one: tall, thin... absolutely *gorgeous*. Her skin is like porcelain. I don't know that I've ever seen anyone with skin quite as perfect as hers. I've asked her about it before and do you know what she uses? Goat's milk. Not moisturizers *made* with goat's milk, mind you, but *actual* goat's milk! Straight from the teat!"

"Oh?" Jonny manages, though Alice doesn't appear to hear him.

152

"Anyway, what was I saying? We were talking about Sophie, weren't we? She paints landscapes, much like I do, but tends toward oils instead of watercolors. Oh, now and again she might work with acrylic, but I think that's fairly unusual these days. She has her own studio. I forget the name of it—it might just be called Fergusons', now that I think about it—but you can find it just outside of town. Check the hours before you drive out there; I'd hate to see you go all that way only to find no one's in. I'm not sure the name of the road they're located on, but both she and her husband work out of a barn. It's painted to look like a rainbow.

"When I say a rainbow, I don't mean they painted a mural on the side of it or anything like that. What they did was paint every slat a different color: red, orange, yellow... Oh, I'm sure you get the idea. You seem like an intelligent young man."

Jonny isn't sure how the artist has come to this conclusion seeing as he's only managed two complete sentences since making her acquaintance. He'd like to voice another sentence now, but unfortunately isn't given the chance. Offering a toothy smile that stretches her rubbery cheeks in a way reminiscent of the Grinch's, Alice Clodham pushes back the brim of her sunhat and continues, "You know, now that I think about it, it's been quite some time since I bumped into either Ansel *or* his wife. I assume they're still in the area, but I suppose it's possible they moved away. Their children are grown now, I imagine; couples often take advantage of that and tend to downsize. Some stay put, but others move away. A lot of folks tend to travel, though when you live in a part of the world as pretty as I do, I don't really see the need to leave.

"It probably sounds odd, seeing as I'm an artist like I am, but travel has never been something that's appealed to me. If you can believe I was ever young, I'll share a story with you. I couldn't have been more than six or seven when it happened. My family lived not too far from here, see, in a little town you'll never have heard of that's located about forty-five minutes north of Radio Park. I come from a big family: five brothers and two sisters. I'll need both hands to tell you their names," she explains, setting her paintbrush in a jar of water balanced there on the easel. She employs a new finger each time she rattles off the name of a sibling: "Agnes, Amos, Jacob and Roy—they were twins—Henry, Julia, and... Oh, who have I missed? Agnes, Amos, Jacob, Roy, Henry, Julia, and... Wesley!" Alice throws her hands in the air, brings them together with a joyful clap. "How could I forget Wesley? He was quiet, sure, but had a heart of pure love. And the reddest hair you've ever seen!

"Funny thing about Wesley, if you don't mind me sharing real quickly, but he never lost all of his baby teeth! How about that? Have you ever heard of such a thing? Wes was eighty-eight years old when he died and he *still* had a baby tooth or two stuck in that mouth of his. I'm not sure why the dentist never pulled them, but I guess if they weren't causing any harm..."

8:53a.m. (PDT)

With Alice Clodham's life story swirling around in his brain, Jonny walks back to his car, climbs inside, and turns the air conditioner on at full blast.

The white noise produced by the vents is music to his ears. He thinks he's probably never experienced anything so beautiful in all his life.

JANE.

The look that slowly spreads across Piper's face as a massive tour bus pulls into her drive and comes to a standstill is one of sheer puzzlement. She'd already been thrown for a loop when Gabby and Reese had shown up at her apartment quite a bit earlier than expected and told her to grab her bathing suit and a towel.

Now, it seems, the mystery of the day has intensified even further.

"What's going on," she demands, eyes dancing back and forth between her cousin and soon-to-be sister-in-law. Marta wears a pinched expression that's not meant to look pinched and a strikingly white monogrammed kimono.

Jane opens her mouth to answer as Kai rounds the house with two of the many inflated innertubes, but before she's able to offer an explanation, the door to the bus opens and Bert Robinson bounds into the sweltering day. "I sure hope everyone's wearing sunscreen!" he says in greeting. "That sun is fuckin' *blazing!*"

Following on his heels are the band's drummer and bass guitarist, Kenny Russo and Finn Gregory, respectively; Sebastian brings up the rear. "Hi Jane," he says in that soft, quiet way of his, the pale iciness of his eyes somehow exuding warmth. His arms go around her, wrapping her in a tight hug, and then he pulls away to consider the rest of the day's participants, plus Ansel and Sophie. Presenting himself in a way not at all suggestive of the truth that "Uptempo, Down" has been, for the second week in a row, the most popular song in the nation, he extends a hand and repeats the name of each person to whom he's introduced. The gesture is sweet; even Marta, despite her uppity exterior, appears awed.

"Let's get this show on the road," Finn says as he takes the tubes from Kai and loads them onto the bus. Then he, Russo, and Bert follow the younger man to the back of the farmhouse, where they retrieve the rest of the rafts and return a few moments later. While they're gone, Bas speaks to Piper about Radio Park, commenting on the uncanny amount of traffic circles and roundabouts the town has to offer. Then, running a hand through his tousled curls, he smiles shyly and wonders, "Seeing as you're letting us crash your bachelorette party, the band and I'd like to take everyone for drinks after tonight's show. You choose the venue; we'll go wherever."

It is when these words are spoken that something seems to register on Piper's face. "Hold on," she commands, her jaw slackening as she turns to gape at Jane. Though she says nothing, every thought in her head is written there on her face: goodbye, spa day; hello, dancing and margaritas! With a squeal, she throws her arms around her cousin and squeezes her tight. "You are too much!" she whispers into her ear. "Thank you, thank you, *thank you!*"

The group makes good time. Sophie sends along an assortment of fruit to eat on the water—watermelon and cantaloupe, blackberries and blueberries—that resides in Tupperware containers nestled among the beer.

Kai and Finn hit it off immediately. Interested in someday covering his body with ink in the same way his father has done, Kai wonders about the intricate pattern covering the bassist's left forearm. Bas and Bert, often inseparable, float side by side on their matching blue tubes. The latter does most of the talking, chattering with the women and recounting exploits from recent shows. "We played Red Rocks last week," he says easily. He doesn't brag about the accomplishment when he shares this. Instead, his tone is laced with amazement... as if he still can't believe he and the band had been invited to perform at such an iconic location. "It was absolutely incredible."

Russo, wearing a ballcap to protect his fair complexion, flirts jovially with Piper's college friend. Lauren is short and fit, with muscular legs that broadcast her love of gymnastics. Her voice, sweet and nearly as high-pitched as Minnie Mouse's, takes a bit of getting used to. The drummer seems smitten by her, though; Jane notes the way he flexes his abs each time he reaches for a fresh beer.

Seeing as this is her first time with the Storm sisters, Jane devotes a portion of the float to conversing with Marta and Maude, and even though Marta is slow to relax into the impromptu agenda, she *does* loosen up a little more with each sip of her pilsner. Maude, on the other hand, is surprisingly fun. Small and slender, she wears her nappy hair in an elegant afro. Her bone structure is striking and her smile is constant; when she laughs, the sound originates in her belly and bubbles straight out of her, echoing across the river and reaching the ears of people standing onshore. "The thing about Max and Marta," she says conspiratorially as she floats beside Jane, a hand trailing beside her in the water, "is that they're both so *uptight* about everything. Maybe it's because I'm the youngest that I don't feel as much pressure to perform, but I don't. I just..." She lifts her shoulders in a dismissive shrug. "...don't. For now, I'm content living paycheck to paycheck and trying to make a name for myself and my store."

Jane thinks back to what Kai had told her about Maude: "She has a part-time gig selling expensive clothes at some lofty shop downtown."

"What is it that you do?" she wonders.

Maude's teeth gleam in the sun as she grins brightly. "So right now I'm the manager of a boutique in downtown Radio Park. We sell bags, jewelry, and one-of-a-kind articles of clothing. Each item is handmade so it's completely unique. My ultimate goal in life is to be able to make a living selling *my* clothing—I went to school for fashion design—so the owner, Beatrix, is pretty cool about letting me hang my work there. It's a nice bonus when something sells, but it's gonna be a while until I'm able to quit my day job!" She laughs, indicating that this is not a real hardship, and adds, "It helps that my boyfriend and I moved in together last year. Making rent has become a lot easier."

"And he's a pharmacist?" Jane confirms, once again summoning information provided by Kai.

Maude giggles, amused. "Um... not quite. Quentin manages one of the Rite Aids over in Bend, and that *does* pay okay, but he is *definitely* not a pharmacist!"

1:01p.m. (PDT)

Piper cups a handful of blueberries in her palm and steadies a bottle of beer between her tanned thighs. "This," she says as her yellow innertube bounces against Jane's, "is so much better than the spa."

"You're having fun?"

"I'm floating down the river with a bunch of really cute rockstars," she says. "Yes, I'm having fun." Her eyes twinkle as she glances at her cousin, the dark lashes elongated by waterproof mascara and the lids shimmery with a faint coating of shadow. Piper wears her long hair in a sloppy knot, the tips wet from being splashed by her brother several meters upstream. Her skin is bronzed and her cheeks are a pleasant shade of pink and the concealer that she normally wears is smudged enough to show off the constellation of freckles beneath her right eye. The coconutty aroma of sunscreen wafts around her.

"Hey, Pipe," Jane wonders, taking a long pull of her beer before voicing her question. "Why is it you've started to cover your freckles?"

Automatically, Piper's free hand flutters up to touch her cheek. Of course she can't feel the faint blemish, but her fingers know right where it is. As they linger there, the corner of her mouth lifts upward in a faint smile. "You won't like the answer," she confides, "but it's because of Max. He has a weird thing about symmetry."

"What do you mean?"

"I mean, he likes things to be symmetrical. When they're not, he's really bothered by it."

Jane supposes that somewhere, maybe in the *DSM*, there is a name for this disorder. She narrows her eyes behind her sunglasses and stares hard at her cousin. "But you're an artist," she points out. "Isn't symmetry sort of frowned upon when it comes to photographing things? That's what my high school art teacher told me, anyway; she said asymmetry is the way to go."

"It usually is, but not this time. Max can be a little bit OCD about things. Sometimes, if I forget to hide my freckles, he'll fixate on them and not be able to focus on what I'm saying. It's just easier to cover them up." She volunteers this information as if it's the most natural thing in the world to have a fiance who can't bear to look at her face unless it's been painted to depict a face that isn't quite hers.

Jane bites her lip and says nothing.

She isn't sure there's anything *to* say.

1:48p.m. (PDT)

"We'll obviously be playing 'Kick It' and 'Uptempo, Down' at tonight's show," Bas says around a mouthful of watermelon, "but d'you have any other requests?"

Jane paddles closer to him, spins her tube so she's facing the quiet frontman. "Nope. This day is already way more magical than I allowed myself to imagine it could be. Play whatever you want; we'll dance to all of it."

"We can make it so you're right in front of the stage," he offers. "When you get there tonight, walk around to the back of the venue. There'll be a bouncer with a list. Me and Bert recorded everyone's names on the bus ride over here; I'll give it to security when we get back to the Post Press and you guys should be good to go."

"Really? Thank you, Bas. You have no idea how much I appreciate this."

"Yeah, sure. It's not a big deal. Thanks for arranging all this," he says with a wave of his hand, indicating the gentle lapping of the water and the brilliant sunshine overhead. "It's nice to get out and do stuff before the show, you know? Yesterday—we were up in Portland, I guess—me, Finn, and B played some minigolf. I lost terribly; golf is definitely not my sport."

Jane laughs. "You're good at other things," she assures him. "Believe me."

Bas blushes and picks at the label of his pale ale. Then, with a voice soft and pure, he sings the opening lyrics of "Goin' Down," an old song by the Monkees, expertly changing the lyrics a bit to make it his own: *Floatin' in the river with a saturated liver / And the water is a-quiver / Blinding sunbeams gleaming above / As we celebrate the true love / Of one Piper and her Maxwell / But tonight we're gonna dance and sing 'til dawn / Until we yawn / 'Til Thursday's gone / And we move on.*

"Keep goin', B!" Bert cheers as he swims up beside him.

162

On the other side of Jane, Gabby and Reese clap animatedly and Piper sticks her fingers in her mouth to execute a piercing whistle. Maude's contagious laugh bubbles out of her, Kai whoops with delight, and even Marta seems impressed with this spontaneous performance.

Cheeks blazing a deep shade of crimson, Bas shakes his head and splashes his feet in the water. "That's all I've got for right now," he chuckles. "There'll be more tonight, though. I promise."

JONNY.

Thursday, 2:12p.m. (PDT)

Having sufficiently rested his ears after his encounter with Alice Clodham, Jonny had ventured back to the public library and searched for the employee who'd been so helpful the day before. "I think you're talking about Theresa," a coworker deduced when he'd described the young librarian with the bun atop her head. He'd smoothed his wispy mustache and added, "She's off today, but maybe I can help you find what you're looking for."

Still exhausted from the abundance of information he'd received first thing that morning, Jonny had attempted to succinctly present the gist of what he was hoping to learn:

- Is there a barn painted to resemble a rainbow somewhere in Radio Park?
- If so, where is it located?
- And is Piper Ferguson a resident of the town?

As it turns out, the local paper had printed an article about the Fergusons' colorful barn well over a decade ago, shortly after the family decided to paint it. In order to read the publication, Jonny and his new librarian friend had been required to wrestle with microfiche, but the men ultimately came out on top. Conveniently, both an address *and* a picture of the bright structure had appeared right there above the fold.

Perhaps more importantly, Jonny had been given access to a phonebook kept behind the circulation desk. In the second column, about a quarter of the way down the page and nestled among Floyds and Fletchers and Farmers and Franks, was an entry for Piper Ferguson. "I found you," he'd whispered aloud to himself as the name came into focus. "I finally have an address!"

He'd jotted the house number and street name on the back of a receipt and carried it out to his car. And then, wasting not a second more than he needed to and arriving at 11:18a.m. on the nose, he'd driven over to 451 James Avenue and knocked at the door.

No one had answered.

Which is why he now sits alone at the bar of a brewery known as the Terrible Terrier, nursing a hazy IPA and picking at an order of fries smothered in beer cheese. "Can I get you anything else?" the bartender asks, sensing his sullenness and offering a sympathetic smile. "You seem glum."

"Oh, I'll be alright," he assures her. "My day's just not going quite as I'd planned. Hey, do you by chance have a sheet of paper and a pen I could borrow?"

"Of course, yeah! Hold on."

She disappears, only to return a moment later with a small notepad and a ballpoint pen. Yellow paper, black ink. He thanks her and pushes his food to the side, uses a napkin to mop up the condensation from his sweating beer. And then he begins to write.

Thirty minutes later, Jonny has managed to compose three somewhat decent-sounding sentences that don't necessarily present him as an obsessive psycho who's just traveled across the country in the hopes of reconnecting with a woman whose full name he only learned a couple hours ago:

> *I'm not sure if you remember that time in Denver when your plane was grounded for several hours and we ended up sharing nachos and conversation at a shady Mexican restaurant. I'm in Radio Park for the next few days and wouldn't mind catching up and splitting another plate of nachos. Give me a call if you'd like to meet up.*
>
> *~Jonny Rockford*
>
> *(252) 555-7019*

When he finishes, at least ten wads of crumpled paper litter the bar, the cheese on his fries has congealed to an unappetizing glob of grease, and his glass is completely empty. "I'll take another IPA," he says when the bartender comes over to check on him. "Thanks."

It's as he's compiling the discarded letters to Piper and placing them on his plate that he feels a warm, moist tongue on his leg. Startled, he glances down to find a massive dog has sprawled itself at his feet and is politely cleaning his shin. "Well, hello there," Jonny chuckles, leaning over to pet the pup's broad head. "Who are you?"

"His name's Boris," the bartender offers as she places a fresh beer on the bar. "He belongs to the owner. I forget what kind of breed he is... Some sort of terrier, obviously." Apparently feeling the need to explain why she hasn't already committed this tidbit of information to memory, she adds, "I only got hired last week. Actually, I wasn't even supposed to be working today, but one of our regular staff members asked to switch shifts with me. His sister's getting married this weekend, I guess, and he needed the day off to get some stuff done." She shrugs to show that she doesn't mind granting the favor.

Jonny nods in acknowledgment and continues scratching Boris's ear. "You don't seem so terrible," he muses. "You're a sweet guy, aren't you?" It occurs to him that he ought to ask another employee about the dog's breed as it's something that will no doubt interest Alex, but even the thought of exerting the effort is exhausting. His heart is heavy, his hand is sore from composing so many drafts of a three-sentence letter, and all he really wants to do is drink his beer in silence.

So that's what he does.

ANSEL.

There's a distinct smell that exists in sporting supply stores: a medley of rubber and plastic and the clean aroma of new sneakers. Ansel fills his lungs with it as he steps inside Hike-Camp-Repeat, allowing his pupils a moment to adjust to the fluorescent lights and his body a moment to adapt to the blustery air conditioning. He's not entirely sure why he's come—he has no need of anything that can be purchased at this particular vendor—but the needle of the compass on his wrist continued to spin throughout the night, and when he'd woken this morning, he'd known in his gut that to stop it would require a trip into town.

And now he's here.

Puzzling over the reason why, he meanders down the narrow aisles and between the overstuffed racks of athletic wear. When his children were younger, Kai especially, he'd bring them here for new shoes at the start of each school year. It's been nearly a decade since he last had to do that, he realizes, and the awareness blankets him with an unexpected sadness.

His thoughts travel to the upcoming weekend and the fact that he'll be losing his little girl to a man who values money and stature more than art and kindness. He hasn't voiced this opinion to Piper, of course, but it's how he feels. Max isn't a bad man, per se, but he's not the man Ansel would have chosen for his daughter. In the brief time that she's been with him, Piper has changed. Her self-esteem isn't quite as high as it had been, her vivacity for life a bit dulled.

Sighing, he pushes these worries from his mind and tries to focus on what needs to be done in the upcoming hours. With his children on the river and his wife shopping for last-minute wedding supplies, they'd made the executive decision not to reopen the studio until Monday morning. What Ansel *should* be doing right now is wiping down the lawn furniture that will be used first for tomorrow night's rehearsal dinner, and later for the backyard reception.

What he's doing wasting time in Hike-Camp-Repeat is a mystery to him. He's about to forfeit the mission and go home when a jovial voice sounds from behind him.

"Well, *there* you are!" the man exclaims, holding his arms so the palms of his hands face the ceiling. "Life's sure a funny thing, ain't it? It was just yesterday, I believe, a young fellow stopped in here asking about that frame shop you used to run. He had quite a few questions about it, he did."

Ansel cocks his head as he studies Xavier Kinney, wondering why on earth someone would come *here* to gather information about You've Been Framed. The storefront has been closed for five years now, at least. And besides that, a frame shop isn't generally the type of business folks tend to remember—even one that incorporated mugshots into its marketing.

"'A young fellow'?" Ansel repeats. He runs a hand over his bald head, scratches his left bicep with calloused fingers. "Who was he?"

"He didn't give me his name, but he wasn't from around here. He couldn't have been; his accent was too thick. Southern. Texas, Georgia... one of the Carolinas, maybe. I can't imagine he came all this way just to have a picture framed, but he was interested in learning about you all the same." Xavier smiles brightly, then promptly allows the wide grin to fall. "He wanted your name, but my memory ain't what it once was. I put him in touch with Alice Clodham expectin' she'd know more about the art world than I. It could be he'll reach out to you in the next day or so."

Rather than reintroduce himself to Xavier Kinney, Ansel excuses himself and heads back to his truck. "Good lord," he mutters as he climbs behind the wheel. "Whoever it is who's looking for me, he's probably *still* with Alice. His ears are likely bleeding by now..."

JONNY.

Thursday, 3:33p.m. (PDT)

Since he doesn't have any tape, Jonny finds a substantially-weighted rock and anchors his three-sentence note to the doormat on Piper Ferguson's front stoop. There's a slight overhang and it rarely rains in this part of Oregon to begin with, so he thinks the setup is safe.

His heart is beating rapidly as he walks back to his rental car and climbs in.

Before driving away, he fishes his cell from his pocket and plugs in the number for the rainbow-painted barn located outside of town. Just as it had when he'd tried calling from the Terrible Terrier, the line rings into oblivion. Neither human nor machine feels inclined to answer.

6:03p.m. (PDT)

"You need cheering up," Artie says when he arrives home earlier than expected later that day, "and fortunately for you, I have just the thing. A coworker of mine had tickets for tonight's show at the Post Press, but something came up and now he can't go. Guess who scored the tickets."

"You?"

"Ding-ding-ding! Now guess who's playing."

"Flannel Lobster," Jonny says, recalling the conversation he'd had yesterday morning with the barista at Cup o' Mud Buzz. "That's a sold-out show. It's gonna be packed."

"And doors open at six-thirty," Artie informs him. "We're already gonna be pushing it to get there on time, but if we hurry, I think we can be there before the opening act goes on. Worst-case scenario: we miss Spanky Angus and make it in time for the headliner."

Despite the downward projectile his feelings have seemed to follow over the course of the day, Jonny snorts and repeats, "Spanky Angus?"

"It's a local act," Artie says with a wave of his hand. "They play a lot of venues in Bend and Radio Park. I like 'em, but I won't be upset if we miss their set. Let's get changed, huh? Maybe we can grab a burger at Mickey D's or something on the way."

7:58p.m. (PDT)

By the time the men enter the Post Press, the venue is full and Spanky Angus is in the midst of saying goodnight. "You've been great, Radio Park!" the drummer screams into his microphone. "You always are! Thanks for having us!"

The trio exits the stage, tossing guitar picks into the front row and sailing a set list that's been folded into a paper airplane over the heads of the crowd. It lands somewhere in the middle; a dip in the surface appears as several folks bend down in the hopes of retrieving it.

"Are you someone who needs to be up front for shows?" Artie asks, leaning into his friend so as to be heard above the music blaring from giant speakers. "I'm fine standing in the back, but if you wanna move closer—"

"The back's fine," Jonny interrupts. "I'm gonna grab a beer. D'you want one?"

"Please!"

Leaving Artie behind to wield his elbows and hold the less-than-impressive spot the men have settled on, Jonny walks over to get in line at one of the bars lining the club's perimeter. As he stands there waiting to place his order, he scans the facility and considers the interesting decor. On the ride over, Artie had explained that the building had originally been used to print Radio Park's local newspaper. When the business relocated to a larger space more than two decades ago, however, a newcomer to the area had purchased the Post Press and turned it into a nightclub. Nowadays, the venue is used several times each week to host concerts of all sorts.

In order to keep with the history of the structure, its walls have been papered with old newspapers and the general color scheme of practically everything within their confines consists of black, white, and grey. The only exception to this is the back wall, which has been painted a bold shade of red. The silhouettes of simplistically drawn houses stand against the scarlet backdrop, as does the outline of a boy on a bike. He wears a satchel overflowing with rolled newspapers and tosses one to each home as he pedals through the neighborhood. The title of the piece, Jonny is informed by the man standing in front of him, is "Black and White and Re(a)d All Over," and despite the childish nature of the pun, it does earn a smile.

Returning with the beer a good fifteen minutes later, Jonny falls in beside Artie just as the lights begin to dim and the stage goes dark.

JANE.

Thursday, 8:23p.m. (PDT)

Having a close friend who dates the lead singer of Flannel Lobster means that Jane has seen the band perform on dozens and *dozens* of occasions.

Nevertheless, each time they take the stage, an electric energy courses through her veins. Her extremities tingle while at the same time becoming paralyzed; she feels the desire to dance, but can't force herself to move until all four men have taken the stage.

They walk out together, breaking apart to claim their respective microphones and instruments: Russo behind the drumset, Finn armed with an electric bass, Bert and Bas on guitar. Every once in a while their frontman will talk to the crowd, but more often than not it's his sidekick who gets the audience pumped up. Now, for example, Bert leans into his mic and says animatedly, "Hey there, Oregonians! We know it's this fuckin' song that you're all here for, so we decided to play it first. Surprise!" And just like that, every set of feet in the whole entire building is jumping along to the uptempo melody of "Uptempo, Down."

Jane grabs hold of Piper and the two jump right along with them.

Afterward, Bas sneaks out to fetch the members of the bachelorette party. The encore's finished and the lights are glaringly bright, but persistent fans linger in front of the stage. "Show's over," security informs them. "Time to go home, everyone." But the small gathering cheers when they catch sight of the frontman, pestering him for pictures and autographs.

Bas smiles shyly, his cheeks growing rosier with each passing second, and politely fulfills his obligation to cater to the fans. Ten minutes is plenty for the bashful musician, however, and he slips away as soon as he's able. Motioning to Jane, he beckons for her and her cohorts to follow him backstage, where the crew and band members are busily winding up cords and securing backup instruments in sturdy cases. "Where are we going next?" Russo wants to know. "We can meet you there or head over together. Is there someplace within walking distance?"

Jane turns to Piper. It's she who should choose the venue.

"How about The Library?" she suggests. "The first floor is a bar and restaurant, but the second floor has dancing and a DJ."

"I'm up for that," Finn says. "Can we walk?"

Kai nods. "It's not far from here."

Jane turns to Sebastian, remembering the menu she'd perused while there the other night with Piper and Max. "I know you're more of a beer and wine guy, but The Library serves a drink called Tequila Mockingbird. I thought of you when I saw it."

Bas grins. *To Kill A Mockingbird* is his favorite book. "I might need to get it, just because."

"I might get one with you."

Friday, 12:18a.m. (PDT)

The only time Piper leaves the dancefloor is when she needs to order another refill of Are You There, God? It's Me, Margarita. For the most part, her friends do their duty and her glass is never empty. Jane watches from the sidelines as she, Gabby, and Reese grind to Usher's "Yeah" and Britney's "Toxic."

When the disc jockey plays "Hey Ya!" by Outkast, all four members of Flannel Lobster—Bas included— surround her and shake their hands as if they're bringing Polaroid snapshots into focus. Maude requests Beyoncé's "Crazy In Love" and then promptly arranges for the entire bachelorette party to surround the VIP as she takes a turn dancing with each of them, and Kai surprises absolutely everyone by busting a move to Missy "Misdemeanor" Elliott's "Get Ur Freak On."

The night concludes with the whole crowd moving to the left, then to the right, and hopping it out together as they "Cha-Cha Slide" their way across the dancefloor. When the last song ends and the lights come on, the silence that ensues feels aggressively loud. Piper throws back her head and releases a mighty laugh, wraps one arm around Jane, the other around Kai, and follows the throng of people downstairs and outside.

A street light casts a warm glow on the sidewalk; moths flutter about the illuminated orb overhead. Now that the sun's gone to bed, the air is chilly, and Jane shivers in the cool evening. Her skin feels sticky and tight, the sweat drying quickly on her bare extremities.

"*This*," Piper says, extending her arms in a way meant to encompass everyone, "has been the absolute *best* bachelorette party I could have ever asked for, *ever*." Though her words aren't slurred, she pronounces them in a way that suggests moderate inebriation. "I wish it could last forever, but it can't, and that's partly because I have to go to bed." She smiles, hiccups, and turns to face the band. "Bas. Bert. Russo. Finn." She fixes each with a smile, nodding her head as she says their individual names. "Thank you for making this day so special. You were one of my favorite bands *before* today, but now you are my *only* favorite band." Piper blows them a kiss, as if this somehow reinforces the statement.

"Well, thanks," Bas says amiably, trying to hide a smile.

"I just think it's really fuckin' neat that we got to be a part of your *bachelorette* party!" Bert exclaims, his grin boyish and joyful. "This was my first one!"

"Not to bum you out, B," Bas mutters in a low voice, "but it'll probably be your last."

Bert seems offended. "Why's that?"

Bas runs a hand over his trim beard and shakes his head. Then he clasps his best friend's shoulder and says, "You know what? I'll explain it on the bus. Jane, thanks for the invite. Piper, congratulations; I hope you have a ton of fun this weekend. Everyone else, it was great meeting you and

178

spending time with you, but we've got a gig in San Francisco tomorrow and we're driving through the night. So... we're out. G'night."

"I'm gonna sleep with you," Piper says, following Jane inside and upstairs to the bedroom that was once hers and now acts as a guest room. "Is that okay? There's no reason for me to go home; I brought everything with me that I'll need for tomorrow."

Jane peels off her silky top and kicks out of her denim skirt. She's brushed her teeth and washed her face, but mascara still clings to her lashes and her armpits smell boozy and sweet. What she should do is hop in the shower, but everyone is meant to be meeting back at the Ferguson residence early tomorrow morning in order to caravan over to Cici's Salon. Manicures, pedicures, and a rehearsal dinner are on the docket for Friday. At some point, she needs to acquire a bit of sleep.

"That's fine," Jane says in answer to Piper's question. "Come on in." She holds up the covers and her cousin, still clad in the slinky green dress she'd been wearing all evening, climbs in beside her.

The women rest their heads on the same pillow, shoulders pressed tight against one another.

"Can I tell you something?" Piper asks. "You have to promise not to judge me."

"You can always tell me something and I will never judge you."

"Yeah, but do you *promise*?"

179

"I promise."

Piper exhales. She hasn't brushed her teeth and her breath is a sweet-sour medley of many margaritas and one late-night order of Lord of the Fries. "Sometimes," she confides in a very tiny voice, "and especially lately, I find myself remembering this guy I met when I was only twenty-one. His name was Jonny and he was from somewhere in North Carolina and he was really, *really* sweet. And cute too. But mostly I liked him because he was sweet."

Jane catches her breath and her heart skips a beat. Could this be the man Kai had told her about on Tuesday night? As casually as she can manage, she prompts, "Where'd you meet him?"

"In Denver. I was coming back from visiting you and my flight was delayed. He was just... on a trip out west, I think. By himself. And we both ended up in the same restaurant at the same time, sitting beside one another at the bar. He bought me a margarita and I shared my nachos with him... and then he actually ended up paying my tab, so I guess Jonny technically shared *his* nachos with *me*." She laughs, an indication that she's never realized this before, and wiggles closer to her cousin. "I really liked him, Janie. He was funny and smart and I caught him staring at my lips all night."

"Did you kiss him?"

Piper shakes her head, the rustle of the pillowcase audible in the quiet room. "I wanted to, but I didn't. I was too scared. He was a few years older than I was. Like, three or four maybe. Not a *big* age difference. Not like Max and me. I just... I felt young next to him. Too young to make a move."

"So how did it end?"

"We hugged. He smelled *so good*. Like basil and rain and fabric softener. I remember his scent really well. It was so unique, you know?"

"It sounds unique," Jane grants, and immediately begins to ponder how she might opt to describe Marcus's aroma. He'll be arriving tomorrow. With any luck, she'll be able to fill her nostrils with his scent in fewer than twenty-four hours.

"Anyway," Piper sighs, rolling over and pressing her back against Jane's side, "that's what I wanted to tell you. Just that I've been thinking about Jonny and wondering how my life would be different if we'd exchanged numbers or something."

Jane bites her lip, asks the question. "Do you wish that you had?"

"Well... then I wouldn't have Max, would I?"

No matter which way one looks at it, the answer is not a "no."

JONNY.

Friday, 6:18a.m. (PDT)

"You're up early."

Dressed in a pair of charcoal slacks and a fitted button-down, Artie leans against the kitchen counter skimming the newspaper. There's a mug of coffee near his left elbow and a pot of coffee on the burner. He watches his friend with concern as Jonny pads across the tiled floor and groggily rummages in the cupboard for a mug, then fills it with the strong brew and slurps a big sip. "I guess Piper didn't call, did she?"

Piper had most certainly *not* called.

Having gone to bed around midnight, Jonny had been unable to sleep. What he should have done was place his phone in his suitcase. Out of sight, out of mind... But what he'd done instead is kept it on his nightstand and checked for new messages every twenty minutes or so.

Alex had texted while on break, just to say that she loved him.

Owen had sent a drunken text with ample misspellings, not saying much of anything.

Even Bruiser, whom he'd not spoken to in ages, had randomly reached out to say "hi."

And yet, the only person Jonny actually cares about hearing from has yet to contact him.

"You know what you oughta do?" Artie poses. "You oughta go off the grid for the day. Go hiking. Explore one of the trails that runs around the base of the Cascades. I mean, let me know where you're going, obviously, so if you get attacked by a mountain lion or something I'll have an idea of where to find your body... but lock your phone in the car and go exploring. Bend is beautiful, Jonny. You're only here for another two days and you've hardly seen any of it."

It's a valid point.

"Alright," he agrees. "I'll do it."

ANSEL.

Friday, 8:32a.m. (PDT)

Although he's sure that his scatterbrained wife *remembers* hanging a sign on
the door to the studio's display room, Ansel isn't entirely sure that Sophie
really *did* what she remembers doing. It is for this reason that he cuts across
the lawn to the barn, mopping his perspiring forehead with a wadded-up
bandana and squinting against the sun.

There's much to be done before tonight's rehearsal dinner, and still more
to be done before tomorrow's main event. He's been up for hours already
and is starting to question how he'll manage to get everything completed
before guests start arriving this evening.

Jane's boyfriend will fly in around two, as will Ansel's sister and
brother-in-law. Their sons and significant others are likely already here,
storing their luggage at the hotel and exploring the town before being able
to officially check into their rooms. His nephews had caught the red-eye, he
knows, and said they'd be available to help with anything and everything
their uncle asked. Ansel had refused their assistance, however, telling them
to enjoy the day, explore Radio Park, and to simply arrive with the rest of
the guests at six o'clock.

As he approaches the barn, it becomes immediately evident there is no sign affixed to the door. He chuckles inwardly, even though this is yet another task he'll need to take care of, and fumbles for his key. Wallace accompanies him, weaving between his legs as he walks to the register and scours the drawers for a sheet of blank paper and a Sharpie. Finding both, he quickly scrawls "On account of family matters, we will be closed until Monday. Thank you for understanding." Then he uses one hand to scoop up the tabby, another to carry the sign and a roll of tape, plops Wallace outside, and quickly adheres the notice to the door. "There," he says to the cat. "If anyone shows up between now and next week, at least they'll understand there's a reason we're not open."

From his perch on the ground, Wallace offers a sing-songy mew before walking away, his tail swishing behind him as he crosses the yard.

JANE.

Friday, 10:02a.m. (PDT)

The thing is, Jane actually detests nail polish. She can handle it on her toes, but hates the way it feels on her fingers. Not only does the chemical smell give her a headache, but the way the polish feels is constricting.

Taut.

Rigid.

Stiff.

A fresh coat of shimmery gloss may not directly affect the brain, but Jane feels she can't think with the polish on her nails. She picks at it constantly. She wants to soak a cotton ball in remover and eliminate the subtle color only minutes after having it applied.

"It really bothers you, doesn't it?" Maude observes as she catches Jane picking at her cuticles. Her tone is light, her smile warm. "I'm used to it. My mom started taking me for mani-pedis when I was still in the single digits. Crazy, right?" Her contagious laugh is bubbly, but the slightest bit subdued. Jane suspects this is because, deep down, Maude understands that children don't need to have their nails professionally cared for.

"It just feels so *tight*," she tries to explain. "I'm not used to it."

"Well, think of it this way: you can take it off tomorrow night. Less than forty-eight hours from now, my brother and your cousin will be married. Welcome to the family, sister!" She pats Jane's shoulder, then gives it a squeeze. "It'll all work out just fine."

Jane wonders if it will.

She'd been slightly intoxicated last night, and so had Piper, but the secret shared about Jonny continues to haunt her. "What if Max *isn't* the one?" she wants to ask of anyone who will listen. "What if this is all moving too fast and Piper's not meant to marry him?"

But of course this isn't something that can be spoken aloud.

Especially now, the day before the wedding.

JONNY.

Friday, 10:35a.m. (PDT)

The weather, only in the seventies at this time of day, is perfect for hiking. Jonny has done as Artie suggested and left his phone in the rental, taking with him a backpack loaded with lunch, water, and his car keys.

Not equipped with actual hiking boots, his intent isn't to climb especially high. He sticks to the lower trails, the sandy paths coating his sneakers with dust. Rarely does he happen upon another hiker; it occurs only twice. The first is a man who looks to be in his fifties. His beard is grey, his walking stick gnarled, and the pack of five dogs that accompanies him is a mixture of shepherds and other herding breeds. "'Mornin'," he says as he approaches. One of his pups—a rough-coated collie—sniffs curiously at Jonny's ankle as she passes. "Katie," the man warns, "come on, now."

That's the extent of the conversation.

The second encounter is another man, about the same age as the first, but this one with only one dog and a fancy-looking camera. He stands on a boulder, pointing his lens in the direction of the snow-capped mountains looming above him. His little dog sniffs around the base of the large rock, periodically putting a pebble in its mouth and then spitting it back out. When the pup catches sight of a new person, his stub of a tail begins wagging, the entire back end of his body wiggling adorably. "You're a happy guy, aren't you?" And then to the dog's owner, "What's his name?"

"That's Willy," the man on the boulder informs him. He wears a pair of round spectacles with a rubbery strap to keep from losing them. His hairline is receding; his forehead seems especially pronounced. "He might lick you to death, but he won't bite. You can pet him, if you'd like."

Jonny squats down. Willy promptly places his dirty paws on the man's chest and runs his smooth tongue over his face. His breath smells like he's been eating mud. "You sure are a friendly guy," Jonny muses as he massages the short, pointed ears.

"He's friendly, alright!" the man chuckles.

"What kind of dog is he?"

Willy is caramel-colored, with a squashed snout and a substantial beard. His wide-set eyes are round and black, and although it's obvious that he's ecstatic to be making a new acquaintance, his face conveys an inaccurate expression of disgruntlement.

"A Brussels Griffon. I got him from a breeder in Lancaster County."

"Pennsylvania?"

"That's right. We're from Maryland, so it wasn't much of a drive. I know the Amish have a bad reputation for operating puppy mills, but the woman I got Willy from was the real deal. A few of her dogs have even been shown at Westminster, if you can believe it!" He seems proud of this fact, and very pleased to have gone about purchasing his pup from a reputable source.

Jonny's thoughts aren't on dogs, however. That mention of the Amish had triggered something in his brain, and though he's not meant to be

189

thinking of Piper Ferguson and the five hours they'd spent together more than half a decade ago, that's exactly where his mind travels.

11:09a.m. (PDT)

He eats his lunch while perched atop his own boulder, basking in the sun. It's cooler here than in town and the warm rays feel good on his skin. As he savors his simple peanut-butter-and-jelly sandwich, his thoughts drift to Denver and Piper...

"The Amish don't use zippers, right?"

Then two hours into the date-that-wasn't-really-a-date, Jonny had come to realize the random questions and topics broached by the woman seated beside him at the bar really and truly *were* random. There was no segue between thoughts, no rhyme or reason as to why she sometimes said what she did. The synapses in her brain fired and she responded. It was as simple as that.

"No zippers, no buckles, no collars."

"What about patterns?"

"I'm guessing no, but I could be wrong."

Piper had licked a bit of salt from the rim of her margarita glass, then run her tongue over her lips. She had the nicest mouth. Jonny had wanted to kiss it, and almost had many times, but couldn't quite manage to muster up the courage.

"How come I've never seen an Amish person with a mustache?"

"Maybe because mustaches are skeezy," Jonny had replied, though he vaguely recalled something about facial hair of the upper lip being associated with the military and knew for a fact that the Amish did *not* participate in the military. He'd kept this tidbit to himself, though, and was glad he did when his drinking companion considerately offered, "In general, I agree with you, but some men actually look halfway decent with a mustache. You'd look alright with one, I think."

"Although I appreciate the compliment, I probably won't be growing one any time soon."

"That's fair," she'd laughed. "You look alright without one too."

Now, as Jonny pulls the crust from his sandwich and uses it to form a crumbly bread ball, it occurs to him that Piper had maybe been studying his mouth too. "Hindsight," he mutters aloud, feeling both sad and annoyed. "I should've kissed her. Where's the Wayback Machine when you need it?"

JANE.

Cinnamon gum.

Pine trees.

Earl Grey tea.

"*This*," Jane decides, "is what Marcus smells like."

She stands on her tiptoes, throws her arms around his neck, and presses her lips firmly against his. Then, pulling back and grasping his shoulders, she smiles up at him and says, "I am so glad to see you! Did you have a good flight?"

"I had a *cramped* flight," he says as he gives his left leg a gangly shake. "One of the downfalls to being tall, I suppose. How are you? Your nails are pretty fancy! How are things going at the Ferguson residence?"

"Unc's a bit stressed about piecing together the dancefloor tomorrow morning, but Aunt Sophie's as laidback as ever. The food for the reception is being catered, you know, so all she really needs to worry about is the rehearsal dinner."

They stand at the revolving conveyor belt, watching for Marcus's luggage. When he spots it, he grabs it by the handle and places it on the floor beside him. Then, wheeling it in the direction of the door, he wonders, "What's the menu for tonight?"

"Crabs."

The single syllable is pronounced in a way that conveys zero enthusiasm.

Jane is not a fan of crabs. In theory, the Old Bay-caked crustaceans sound appealing. She likes the idea of sitting outside, surrounded by family and friends, everyone gathered around a table spread with yesterday's news... She likes the little wooden mallets that are sometimes needed to crack a shell, and the way a cold beer has the ability to cool a fiery tongue. Much of what accompanies the consumption of crabs is appealing to her. It's the actual *picking* of the crabs that she dislikes.

"You'd think," she continues, "that Max's family could have chosen something that wouldn't put our manicures at risk. But, no... Instead, they opted for one of the most expensive things capable of being shipped to the desert."

Marcus smiles down at her, amusement glinting in his eyes. "I didn't realize you were such a diva, Janie! The Storm sisters must be rubbing off on you, eh?"

She blushes, realizing just how ridiculous her concern is in the overall scheme of life, and leads the way to her Aunt Sophie's car. Popping the trunk, she grumbles, "Crabs just aren't my thing. That's all. I'm sure it'll be fine."

Marcus loads his luggage into the back of the vehicle, then climbs into the front. As his girlfriend navigates the distance between Redmond and

Radio Park, he wonders about the evening's guest list and asks if Jane has already met everyone who will be in attendance.

"With the exception of Marta and Maude, I haven't been introduced to anyone on Max's side. I mean, unless you count Kai, which I don't, but he *is* one of the groomsmen. He'd prefer not to be, I think, but Max asked him and he couldn't say no."

"That makes sense, though. Like, if you and I were planning a wedding, I'd ask your brothers to be my groomsmen."

"You would?"

"Sure! I like Patrick and Chris."

"Who else would you ask?"

"Mike," he says, naming his own brother, "and probably Zach. What about you?"

This is a game Jane has played many times before with her cousin. She's prepared with her answer. "Piper, Lucy, and Kathryn."

"You need a fourth."

"Why?"

"Because I have four."

"I don't want a fourth," Jane tells him. "Piper, Lucy, and Kathryn are my very best friends."

"Fine, then I'll drop Zach."

She laughs. "It's not as if we need to decide right now. Unless I slept through a proposal and misplaced a ring, we're not engaged. And there's no rush!" she hastily adds.

Marcus glances over, his smile wide and goofy. "But you *would* like to marry me?" he confirms.

"At some point? Yes, I'd like that very much!"

He reaches over and lifts her right hand from the steering wheel, twining his fingers through hers. "Good to know. I'll keep that in mind."

6:21p.m. (PDT)

Upon meeting the rest of the Storm family, Jane can sort of understand what Maude meant when she talked about the pressure her older siblings feel to succeed. Both Maxwell Terrence Storm, II, Esq. and his wife, Gloria, are intimidating in their own right.

Mr. Max, as Piper refers to him, is a short man who seems tall. His shoulders are broad, his neck thick, and his voice a brash boom that drowns out the conversations of others. Even though the setting is casual, he wears an expensive suit (sans tie) and several gold rings on his fingers. He's handsome in the same way his son is: chiseled features, perfectly groomed, dark eyes that exude confidence. Skin the color of black coffee. His wife, contradictorily, is both taller and plumper than he.

Gloria towers a good four inches over her husband, and while she's not fat, she is wide. "Buxom" is the word that comes to mind when Jane studies her; the woman has curves everywhere. Even her lips are curvier than they should be, suggestive of a recent botox injection. Her skin as a whole is pale, but the concealer she wears on her face provides a complexion reminiscent of creamsicles. When she smiles, the gesture is confined to her mouth. Her gaze carries with it an aura of judgment.

Max's groomsmen, on the other hand, are fairly enjoyable. Jane finds herself listening in on the conversations had by Coop, Cyd, and Jerome. These are the three who had gone through law school with Max and as they suck crab meat from expertly cracked claws, they recount humorous anecdotes of their lives as early twenty-somethings. At one point she finds herself standing beside Cyd at the keg, both of them in need of a refill at the same time and exchanging pleasantries while taking turns filling their cups.

"I heard you revamped the bachelorette party and provided everyone with a real night to remember," he says admiringly. "I'm not much of a Flannel Lobster fan, but I'll admit I'm jealous that you not only got to catch their show, but partied with 'em beforehand *and* afterward. They're nice guys, I gather?"

"The nicest," she assures him, "and definitely worth seeing live."

"Sounds like I missed my opportunity this time. They're heading down the coast right now, aren't they? Not up it? I'll have to catch 'em on their next go-around." He motions for Jane to put her cup under the nozzle and siphons the heady brew into the container. "So you and Piper are cousins?"

"That's right."

"And you've been in town all week?"

"She has!" says a voice from behind, and when Jane turns, she finds Max is also in the market for a refill. He smiles that striking smile of his, gives her arm an affectionate nudge with his elbow. "I imagine she'll say the trip's highlight so far has been Thursday night, but Piper and I managed to introduce her to a few notable restaurants."

It occurs to Jane that Max is in competition with her. He feels threatened by the fact that she succeeded in executing the most memorable bachelorette party her cousin could have asked for and is now trying to prove himself capable of delivering similar levels of fun. This sort of behavior might make a bit of sense if it were being exhibited by Marta, the one whose position of organizer she had essentially usurped, but to witness such insecurity from Piper's fiance is completely unexpected. Jane feels sorry for him, which is likely why she shares, "Max bought me a really nice dinner at The Library. Have you been? The cocktails and food are all named after literature. It's very clever!"

The compliment resonates with Max; his chest swells like a rooster's before it's about to crow. "We went to Olé as well, which isn't nearly as extravagant, but the guacamole *is* some of the best around. Piper loves it there; if given an option, she'll choose Olé every time."

"The boys and I are in town until Monday," Cyd says. "Maybe we'll have to check 'em out."

He excuses himself then, heading back over to reclaim his seat between Coop and Jerome, but Max hangs back for a moment and turns to Jane. "What you did for Piper? Getting in touch with the band and arranging for them to go rafting? The concert and the dancing and the bottomless margaritas? All of it was really incredible, Jane, and I know Piper had a wonderful time. Thank you for treating her to the bachelorette party that she deserved and not the one my sister had planned for her. Marta means well, but she doesn't always hit the nail on the head."

Jane lifts her beer to her lips, takes a small sip. "Of course, yeah. I'd do anything for Pipe."

"I know you would, as would I."

He nods once, his dark eyes suddenly glassy, and quickly looks away. The appearance of tears comes as a surprise. Until right this moment, Jane hadn't witnessed an emotional side to Max. Now, seeing that he has one, she reaches over and lightly rests her fingers on his forearm to recapture his attention. It's in a joking tone that she says, "I'll be watching your moves on the dancefloor tomorrow night. If you can prove yourself to me, maybe I'll invite you to tag along to the next concert. Flannel Lobster's nothing if not danceable."

Maxwell Terrence Storm, III, Esq. grins shyly and blinks the excess moisture from his eyes. "I think I'd like that very much."

ANSEL.

Ansel stands in his bedroom, looking out his window and studying the party occurring in his backyard. He'd popped upstairs to change his shorts. Someone had spilled a cup of beer and the golden liquid had trickled over the lip of the table to saturate the cotton covering his lap. Not wanting to be damp *or* tempted by the aroma of alcohol, he'd excused himself from the festivities and slipped inside. Now, having been awake since about five o'clock this morning, he's trying to muster the energy to rejoin his guests.

From his vantage point, he sees his niece conferring with Max and one of his law-school friends by the keg. They seem to be getting along well; Jane has a tendency to talk with her hands and he can see that the friend, Cyd, is captivated by this.

At a nearby table, Sophie picks crabs with Gloria and her husband. Ansel's brother-in-law, Alan, is seated there as well, as are his nephews, Chris and Patrick, along with their significant others. Marcus can be spotted a bit farther away, laughing with a few of Piper's bridesmaids.

Though he's only had the privilege of being in Marcus's company a handful of times, Ansel has found that the young man has the ability to draw anyone into a conversation. He likes him, despite not knowing him well, and can't help but wish that his own daughter had found someone with similar traits.

"Not that Max *isn't* a good guy," Ansel reminds himself. "He is."

Downstairs, the back door swings open and the sound of footsteps can be heard moving toward the front of the house. His sister's voice drifts up the stairwell, talking animatedly with whoever accompanies her. "More ice," he's able to make out, and "Another roll of..."

Taking a deep breath, he exits the room and hurries down the steps.

Kai stands in the doorway to the kitchen, a roll of paper towels tucked under each arm. "Hey, Dad," he says when he catches sight of Ansel. "Aunt Dot says we need more ice. Is there another bag in the freezer downstairs, or should we just use what's in the ice maker?"

"The keg's fine," Dot explains, "and so is the cooler with all the water and soda, but Sophie put the wine in that long flower box and there's no insulation. I don't want the whites to get warm. The reds, obviously, are fine."

Ansel nods to show his understanding and absently rubs a finger across his right wrist. He can feel the inked needle inching its way around the compass. Glancing down, he sees that it now points in the direction of the barn... which reminds him that their studio cat hasn't yet received his evening meal. "Kai," he says, turning his gaze on his son. "Would you do me a favor and feed Wallace? Dot can take those paper towels outside and I'll run down to get the ice. There should be another bag or two in the basement."

Kai moves his head in a way that results in his dark bangs fanning across his forehead. "Sure," he agrees, passing the rolls of Bounty to his father. "I can do that." He disappears out the front door and strides across the dusty lawn, weaving his way between the many cars that are parked there.

Dot, her strawberry locks the same color as her daughter Jane's but worn in a short bob instead, turns to her brother. "So," she begins in a hushed voice, "Max's mother is a force to be reckoned with, isn't she? 'Frigid' is a word I might use to describe her."

"She's probably my least favorite member of the family," Ansel admits, and then immediately looks around to confirm that they're alone.

Dot laughs, but quickly turns serious. "What are your feelings regarding Max?"

"I take it you're referring to the younger of the two."

"I think you know that I am."

Sighing, Ansel drags a hand across his coarse beard and closes his eyes. "Honestly, Dorothea?" Only rarely does he use her full name, but when he does, it's indicative of the fact that he's about to be brutally honest:

- The summer they'd visited Nantucket for the entire month of July and his sister, only thirteen at the time, had fallen head over heels with an eighteen-year-old who seemed not at all bothered by the age difference: "Honestly, Dorothea, I think the last thing you want to do is get involved with someone who doesn't seem to have much regard for the law."

- That time in their twenties when she'd come for a visit and her hair had not only been bleached, but also permed and teased: "Honestly,

Dorothea, I think you ought to consider shaving your head. Either that, or wear a hat for the next three to six months."

- Three decades ago when he'd refused a glass of wine that she'd offered and then sat her down at the kitchen table, taking her hands in his and hanging his head, ashamed to have kept his secret from her for so long: "Honestly, Dorothea, I've been attending meetings for the last four months; I have a problem."

Dot looks at him now, arms crossed and eyes tinged with worry. "Honestly, Ansel."

"He's not who I'd have chosen for Piper, but she thinks she loves him. Who am I to say whether or not she really does?" He shrugs, shifts the paper towels that he's tucked under his left arm, glances again at the compass pointing towards the barn. "I should get back to the party. I've already been gone too long. I'll grab that ice and meet you outside."

JONNY.

Friday, 6:24p.m. (PDT)

Feeling dirty and tired from a long day of hiking, Jonny glances once more at the phone occupying his cup holder. He'd trekked several miles farther than he'd intended, rationalizing that the longer he distanced himself from his cell, the more likely it would be that he'd return to find a message from Piper.

The logic, not surprisingly, had been faulty.

Piper had not called.

"Damn it," he'd said to the empty car, the words much louder than he had intended them to be. At that point, he'd been angry. He'd traveled nearly three thousand miles in the hopes of reconnecting with someone he'd known for only five hours, and after all that he'd been through to find her, he couldn't very well justify leaving Oregon without giving it one last try.

This is why he'd returned to Radio Park rather than drive back to Bend.

This is why he now pulls up to the curb outside Piper Ferguson's apartment at 451 James Avenue for the second time in two days, marches straight up to her front stoop, and is about to pound his fist against the door when he notices the note he'd written yesterday and anchored to her mat with a rock is still there. He squats to retrieve it, the muscles in his legs screaming after such a long hike. "At least this explains why she hasn't called," he thinks, "but what the hell do I do now?"

6:38p.m. (PDT)

Obviously, he tries phoning before driving the whole way out to the rainbow barn that Alice Clodham had told him so much about. The line rings and rings, though. Not even an answering machine acknowledges his attempt to reach the artists who work there.

Alice had made it sound as though the Fergusons' studio was a fair distance from town, but in actuality it only takes about fifteen minutes to reach it. The lined pavement that Jonny follows eventually becomes unlined, and shortly after that, the road consists of more gravel than asphalt. Admittedly, he *feels* farther from the hustle and bustle of Radio Park than he actually is, but the drive itself isn't difficult in the slightest.

He hasn't brought along the address, but he doesn't need it: the barn looms on his left, a striking conglomeration of colors standing majestically against the mountainous backdrop. He wonders how painstaking and time consuming it must have been to climb up and down such a tall ladder, over and over again, armed with a different shade of paint on each return trip. Respect is what he feels for whoever completed the task, whether it be Piper or her parents or a person they hired off the street, but he's also respectful of the idea. Never in a million years would Jonny have thought to utilize seven colors when painting the exterior of a barn. The fact that someone had not only had the idea but also executed it is impressive to him; while he may not be especially artistic, he certainly has an appreciation for those who are.

The car radio is on, but the volume is low. Nevertheless, the opening chords of Flannel Lobster's recent hit can be heard over the crunch of pebbles, and for the first time, Jonny pays attention to the lyrics. He knows the chorus, of course—it seems the whole world ought to know the chorus by now—but never, until right this moment, has he paid any attention to the song's beginning: "*'Life's what you make of it,' that's what they say. / 'Don't put off 'til tomorrow what's better today.'*"

With the dayglo digits on the dashboard indicating the approach of seven o'clock, Jonny is surprised to find so many cars parked outside the barn. "*'Change that frown to a smile!' 'Carpe diem each hour!' / The truth is all rainbows need sun and a shower.*"

He pulls in beside a grey SUV, shifting into park but not turning off the engine. From the speakers, Flannel Lobster continues to sing, "*Life's just a pogostick: up, down, around. / And at some point you know that you're gonna hit ground.*"

It's not until after the first chorus has been sung—"*Fast is fast and slow is slow; / You need both speeds to make life go. / Reprieves are nice, but so's gusto: / A minute down, then uptempo!*"—that he pulls the key from the ignition and exits the car.

As Jonny approaches the barn, the sounds of laughter and classical music filter in on a gentle breeze. He tunes his ears, trying to determine the source of the noise... wonders if it might be coming from the backside of a nearby farmhouse. This would explain all the cars; perhaps the studio is closed because the Fergusons are having a party.

There's a sign on the door, the bold letters printed with a black Sharpie: "On account of family matters, we will be closed until Monday. Thank you for understanding."

Although Jonny Rockford is not someone who cries easily, he feels as though he is on the brink of tears. By Monday, he'll be back in Moonglow, North Carolina... probably breaking up with Alex because if he's learned one thing from this trip, it's that he's not as invested in the relationship as he'd originally thought.

He drags a hand across his eyes, wiping away the excess moisture, and is debating just how much of a faux pas it would be to crash a stranger's backyard barbecue when the sound of a cat mewing reaches his ears.

Seconds later, a grey tabby is wrapping itself around Jonny's feet.

"Wallace?" a male voice calls. "Where'd you go?"

Jonny turns to find a young man rounding the corner of the barn. He carries a bag of treats in one hand, shaking them like a maraca in an effort to capture the cat's attention. An assortment of keys hangs from his belt loop and jangles musically with each step. "Oh, hey," he says when he catches sight of the customer. "I didn't realize anyone was here. Are you—" his eyes dart to the sign adhered to the barn door "—here to check out the studio? Because we're actually closed at the moment."

The boy is tall and slim, with insanely green eyes and dark hair the same color as coffee beans. If he's not Piper's brother, he should be. The two could practically be twins.

Jonny bends down to scratch Wallace behind the ears, then straightens up, meets the emerald gaze of the boy, and says as calmly as he can manage, "I'm looking for Piper Ferguson. This is going to sound crazy, but I met her six years ago at a bar in Denver and I've spent this entire week trying to find her. I'm only in town until tomorrow evening, and while I understand that you and your family are in the middle of a party right now, I'd *really* like to talk to her. Is there any way you could—"

"You're him," the boy interrupts. "You're the surfer."

Something catches in Jonny's throat. She'd told her brother about him.

"You are, aren't you? I'm right."

He nods. "I do surf, yeah."

The boy grins and switches the bag of cat treats to his left hand so he can use his right one to shake Jonny's. "I'm Kai," he volunteers.

"Jonny," Jonny says.

"Jonny," Kai repeats. "*That's right.* I'd forgotten." His eyes twinkle, then grow dim as his gaze flits toward the farmhouse. "Piper's actually... Well... Just wait here while I get her, okay? I'll be right back."

6:55p.m. (PDT)

Kai doesn't actually return, but a few minutes after he disappears, the front door of the farmhouse opens and a woman wearing a teal dress steps onto the porch. She lifts a hand to her forehead, shielding her eyes from the setting sun, and looks in the direction of the barn. A moment later, she is moving toward Jonny, her silhouette becoming more and more clear with each step.

Piper is almost exactly as he remembers her: dark brown hair, mesmerizing green eyes, and an intriguing look about her that offers only the slightest hint of what sorts of thoughts are taking place inside her head. The only immediate difference is a lack of freckles on her right cheek. Jonny wonders if she had them removed.

He wonders if freckle removal is even an option.

She stops a few feet in front of him, tilting her head to one side and causing her cascade of hair to fall over one shoulder. It's impossible to know what her brother has told her, but it's evident he hadn't included the name of the mysterious visitor. It takes her a moment to place him, but when she does, her face brightens and the two syllables that fall from her mouth sound as though they're accompanied by a thousand exclamation points. "Jonny!"

"Piper," he whispers. "Hi."

ANSEL.

Friday, 11:41p.m. (PDT)

"I know you well enough to be able to tell when something's wrong."

Ansel stands in the doorway of the living room, leaning against the jamb and observing the way his daughter stares blankly into space. Her hands are wrapped around a mug of tea, but no wisps of steam swirl to the ceiling. It could be cold by now; she might have been holding it for hours. The last of the guests left around nine o'clock, departing with enthusiastic promises to return the following afternoon. Except for the bridesmaids, that is, who will convene early tomorrow morning at one of the salons in town to have their hair pinned up and their makeup applied.

Having a delayed reaction to her father's appearance, Piper slowly turns her head to consider him.

"You've been a little bit off ever since Kai pulled you away from dinner earlier this evening," Ansel states. He moves over to sit beside his daughter on the couch. "What's going on, Piper? There's definitely something weighing on your mind."

A lone tear slips through her lashes and slides down her cheek. "I think," she says in the smallest of voices, "that I may be about to make the biggest mistake of my life."

"In marrying Max, you mean?"

She nods. "But I'm equally terrified to call off the wedding because what if *that* ends up being the biggest mistake of my life?" As if she's no more than five years old, she scoots across the couch cushion and snuggles up against her father, allowing him to encompass her with his big arms and press his bristly cheek against her forehead. "Do you remember way back to a whole bunch of years ago when I told you about the man I shared nachos with during a layover in Denver?"

Ansel nods. He does have a faint memory of this. "He was a teacher, wasn't he?"

"Yeah."

"Whatever became of him? Do you know?"

She buries her face in his chest. "I do," she whispers, and then proceeds to recount what had happened when, unbeknownst to the rest of her wedding party picking crabs in the backyard, she had hopped aboard the Wayback Machine to travel six years into the past.

JONNY.

Friday, 11:45p.m. (PDT)

Dumbstruck, Artie stares at his friend. "So you found her?"

"I did."

"And what happened?"

They're sitting on the upstairs balcony of the townhouse, sharing a celebratory beer. Artie has only been home for about ten minutes. The men had spoken tentatively about meeting up with some of Artie's coworkers that evening, but when Jonny had extended his hike by about six miles, he'd texted his friend and told him to go on without him—that if he was feeling up to it, he'd track them down later.

He hadn't felt up to it.

He hadn't, in fact, really known how he'd felt.

If he's being honest, he still doesn't.

There was a sense of elation that came with seeing Piper again. A euphoric warmth that spread through his body and caused his heart to beat double-time. But following that there'd been a sense of dread upon learning she was engaged to be married... and that the ceremony was scheduled to occur the following afternoon.

Artie, growing impatient, knocks his beer against Jonny's knee and arches his brows. "So? What happened? What'd she say?"

"We only talked for about ten minutes."

"Okay...?"

"After that night, she tried to track me down. She got online and visited the websites for dozens and dozens of schools in North Carolina. But she didn't know my last name or my district or which town I lived in... and so she eventually gave up."

"Alright, that's promising. What else?"

"She told me she's been thinking about me a lot lately."

Artie sits up straighter and opens his arms. He's as excited as he'd be if his favorite quarterback had just scored a touchdown with only seconds left on the clock. "Lately? Like, she legitimately said 'lately'? That sounds serendipitous, dude! She's been thinking of you *lately* even though the last time she saw you was *six years ago*. Tell me that's not serendipitous."

As much as Jonny would like to match his enthusiasm, he can't. "And then she told me that she's getting married tomorrow."

"Oh."

Like air released from a balloon, the excitement he'd been feeling seeps right out of Artie. It puddles around him on the floor as he slumps in his chair. "You're shitting me."

"I wish."

"Huh." He chews the inside of his cheek, narrows his eyes. "So how'd you end it?"

ANSEL.

Friday, 11:59p.m. (PDT)

"He kissed me," Piper says, and even though Ansel isn't looking at her, he knows that her cheeks are burning. Not because she's never talked to her father about men before, but because being unfaithful isn't something she's used to. "And I kissed him back... on the eve of my wedding."

Despite himself, Ansel grins.

Despite himself, he has to ask, "And how was it?"

Piper slips a hand behind his back, wraps another across his front. It's been a long time since she's held him this tightly, and an even longer amount of time since she's needed to be held every bit as tight. In a voice that's both dreamy and anguished, she admits, "Magical. It was magical, Daddy. It was the best kiss I've ever had in my life."

"And?"

She sighs and pulls away, reaching for the cup of cold tea that now sits on the coffee table. "And he told me if I change my mind—and if I want to make my getaway—he'll be waiting at the Courthouse Diner bright and early tomorrow morning. He promised to buy me a stack of pancakes so I can drown my sorrows in syrup."

The gesture is a sweet one, and with nothing much to substantiate it, Ansel suspects he would very much like Jonny the educator. With a big hand, he reaches over and smooths his daughter's long hair. "Whatever you decide, Piper? It's going to be the right decision. But promise me one thing, would you?"

"Hmm?"

"Promise to follow your heart."

Saturday, 12:07a.m. (PDT)

Moving quietly so as not to wake his wife, Ansel crosses his bedroom and enters the bathroom. He showers in the dark, washing the day from his skin and leaving his clothes in a pile on the floor. They'll be there in the morning; he'll take care of them then. It could be, after all, that he'll have quite a bit of free time tomorrow.

As he climbs into bed beside Sophie, he extends his right arm far enough to catch a beam of moonlight filtering in through the window. The compass, busily circling for several days now, resides in its normal location: facing north. Although Ansel has no idea what this means, he does understand that what will come will come. At this point, it's out of his control.

JANE.

Jane, snuggled in Marcus's arms for the first time all week, isn't immediately sure what's awakened her. She'd been in the midst of a dreamless sleep when something disturbed her, pulling her from her slumber and forcing her back to reality. She rolls groggily onto her side, rubs at her left eye, and squints at the glowing digits of the alarm clock beside her bed. She still has twenty-two minutes to sleep.

"Janie!"

Her name is somehow both a shout and a whisper. Lifting her head from the pillow, she peers through the dimly lit room and realizes someone is speaking through a narrow crack in the door. "Janie! *Psst!* I need you. Please?"

"Piper?"

"Come out here, would you? I need to talk to you. *Now.*"

Finding her slippers, Jane tiptoes across the room and steps into the hallway, shivering against the cool morning air. She's clad in nothing but a pair of cotton shorts and a tank top. Her nipples are like headlights against the tight fabric; goosebumps quickly cover her arms and legs. "What's the matter?" she whispers. "I thought our hair appointment wasn't until nine."

215

"It's not."

"Then why am I awake now?" For the first time, Jane really studies her cousin. Piper's eyes are rimmed with red and her skin is splotchy. It's obvious she's been crying. It's *possible* she's been crying all night. "Hold on. What's the matter? Why are you—"

"I'm not going through with it," she says in a shaky voice. "I can't. I have too many doubts."

"Wait. Back up. You're not going through with *the wedding*?"

Piper pulls the sleeve of her sweatshirt over her hand and uses it to dab at the dampness on her cheeks. "Everyone is going to hate me, I know, but I can't marry him, Janie. Not after yesterday. Not after Jonny—"

"Jonny? As in... Jonny from Denver?"

"He was here. Last night. And he—"

"I am so confused right now, Pipe. Please slow down. Jonny, the guy you told me about for the first time on Thursday night and hadn't seen for *six years* just randomly showed up last night at your house?"

"Yes."

"And?"

"He kissed me and—"

"He did?"

"—and I'm not saying I love him or anything like that. I hardly know the guy, Janie. But I can't... I can't marry Max if a guy who I've only ever spent a handful of hours with is making me second-guess my decision this strongly. So I need you to cover for me. To explain that I got cold feet and that I just need some time and—"

"Hold on. Back up for a second. Where are you going?"

"I'm meeting Jonny at the Courthouse."

"At the *courthouse*? What're you gonna do, *marry him*? You literally just said—"

In the midst of all her tears and her frantic explanation, Piper begins to laugh. The melodic sound is a welcome one, like sleigh bells announcing joyful carolers or a lullaby right before bed. The sound is happy, and even though Jane doesn't understand why she's doing it, in no time at all she's laughing right along with her cousin.

They're quiet about it. In the room right behind them, Marcus doesn't stir. Neither does Kai, who's tangled in his sheets down the hall, snoring softly into his pillow.

The women double over, clutching their bellies and covering their mouths and eventually squatting low, hands flat against the floor, as they gasp and gasp, attempting to regain control of their breathing. And finally, when Piper is once again able to form words, she says simply, "The Courthouse is a diner downtown. We're going to get pancakes."

"Oh," Jane snorts, wiping moisture from her cheeks. "A diner."

"A diner," Piper repeats. "Yeah." Her green eyes, their lashes sticky with salt, find Jane's and hold them for a long moment. "Do you think I'm a horrible person? Do you think I should—"

"Follow your heart?" she predicts. "Trust your gut?"

Piper nods.

So does Jane. "I do, yeah. I absolutely do. And Piper?"

"Yeah?"

"You are absolutely *not* a horrible person."

JONNY.

Jonny doesn't honestly expect her to come, but since he said he'd be occupying a booth as early as six o'clock, he'd gotten up before the sun in order to fulfill his promise. He's been occupying one of the Courthouse Diner's corner booths for going on two hours. Three cups of coffee have only added to his jitteriness.

His hand trembles as he turns the page of *The Devil in the White City*. His focus is nil. Having read the same paragraph four times without comprehending it, he gives up and moves on. He should just about be an expert on the 1893 World's Fair by now.

He definitely isn't.

A shadow falls across the table and Jonny glances up, prepared to tell the waitress he'll take another refill, but could he please switch to decaf. This request is never voiced, however, because it's not a diner employee who stands at the end of his booth. It's Piper.

"Hi," she says.

Her hair hangs loose, unbrushed but still glossy. He can tell that the previous night, much like his, had been sleepless: her eyes are puffy and pink, her cheeks flushed and feverish. The smattering of freckles, he notes, is still exactly where it had been all those years ago... a constellation beneath her right eye. She wears mesh shorts and a grey hooded sweatshirt, her hands hidden in the kangaroo pocket. When she removes them, the first thing Jonny notices are her sparkly nails. The second, a lack of engagement ring. "You came," he says.

Without a word, she slides onto the bench across from him, her foot accidentally bumping his beneath the table. Jonny holds his breath, closes his book. "I didn't know if you would."

"Neither did I." She bites her lip, holding it tightly between two rows of perfectly straight teeth. Did she wear braces as a child? Jonny has no idea. "I'm not really sure what I'm doing here," Piper continues. "I guess... I guess I just need to know."

He waits, and when she doesn't elaborate, prompts, "Know...?"

"More about you, I guess? I don't even know your last name."

"It's Rockford. Jonathan Charles Rockford."

"Do you still teach eighth-grade social studies?"

"Mmm-hmm."

"Where?"

"Moonglow School District in Moonglow, North Carolina. Our mascot is a seagull."

One corner of Piper's mouth quirks upward. "What's your family like? Do you have siblings?"

"My parents are divorced. My mom, Adelle, lives a few miles from me. After the divorce, my dad—he's in the construction business; his name's Roger—moved to Charlotte. And I've got two brothers. Stevie and Darren.

One's in Virginia, the other moved to Florida. They both teach high-school math." He reaches for his coffee, remembers that it's empty, and instead rests his hand on top of his book. "What about you?"

"Both of my parents are artists: my mom paints, my dad is a woodworker. And my brother Kai, whom you've met, is in school for graphic design." She picks up the laminated menu on the table and picks at its rounded corner. "My full name is Piper Astoria Ferguson."

"Astoria's a city in Oregon, isn't it?"

She nods. "Legend has it that's where I was conceived." Piper's cheeks, already rosy, darken a hue. She lifts her gaze, piercing Jonny with those pure, green eyes. "It might end up that what happened in Denver can't be replicated, you know. There's a lot we don't know about each other. I don't want you to think—"

"I don't," he assures her. "I don't think that at all; I understand this might be it. After today, we may never see each other again. But Piper?"

"Yeah?"

"Can we please exchange numbers this time? Please?"

She laughs. The sound is a mix of happy and sad, hopeful and fearful. "I'll make you a deal," Piper says. "If you buy me a stack of pancakes with a side of *really* crispy bacon, I'll give you my number. Okay?"

"Okay," Jonny agrees. "I can do that."

ANSEL.

Saturday, 11:47a.m. (PDT)

It falls on Ansel to inform Max of the cancellation, and even though he's never been a huge fan of his daughter's fiancé, the task is one of the most difficult things he's ever had to do. Afterward, it takes everything in him not to arm himself with a Solo cup and head outside to drink the dregs of the keg.

He goes to a meeting instead.

And then he sits with his family around the dining room table, sipping a glass of lightly sweetened blackberry tea and picking at leftovers from last night. Kai, Jane, and Marcus still wear their pajamas; the rest of the Montgomery clan is clad in shorts and tees. Everyone's there: Dot and Alan, Chris and Patrick and their significant others... Sophie's parents, who had left the house before receiving their daughter's call and therefore drove in from Bend. Despite the shock that all of them feel, there's also an air of relief. "I never liked the guy," Kai says flatly, speaking from behind an ear of corn. A buttery kernel clings to his unshaved chin. "I'm glad they broke up."

"Have they actually *broken up*?" Marcus wonders, directing the question to Jane. "I was under the impression that Piper hasn't spoken to Max yet."

"She hadn't at the time that *I* spoke with Max," Ansel says, "but I can't imagine there's a different route their relationship will take." What he does not add is his belief that the blow to the lawyer's ego will likely be unforgivable. "I think," he contributes instead, "that Max really did love her... just not in the way Piper needed."

"Right. But did Piper love *him*?" Chris asks. "I'm merely putting the question out there; I obviously don't know the guy. It just seems to me that you don't leave someone at the altar if you're really in love with him."

"There's a difference between loving someone and being in love," Jane points out. "Piper loved Max—she probably will for a while—but she's not *in love* with him. Even if nothing else comes of her breakfast with Jonny, at least she's learned that."

Kai sets the thoroughly gnawed corn cob on his plate and reaches for a crab. "What d'you mean?"

"She means that Jonny may simply be serving a purpose," Sophie explains. "That this might be the universe's way of teaching your sister it's okay to take her time, and that there's no rush to jump into something that she's not one-hundred-percent confident about."

"But I really *like* Jonny," Kai says. "He's cool."

Ansel wraps his hands around his iced tea and smiles at his son. "You don't know Jonny, Kai."

"And you only think he's 'cool' because he's a surfer," Jane points out.

"Admittedly, surfers *are* cool," Patrick's girlfriend chimes in.

Patrick, agreeing with this sentiment, bobs his head up and down.

Later, once Dot and Alan have gone back to their hotel and the cousins have driven into Bend to hike Black Butte Trail, Ansel joins Sophie in the kitchen and slips his arms around her waist. She's standing at the counter, jotting notes on a lined sheet of paper. "At this point, I think I've found homes for all the flowers and food," she sighs. "The caterer is going to deliver the meal to the homeless shelter later tonight and the florist is able to refund a portion of our money because they've managed to sell a few of the bouquets. I just spoke with her a little while ago." She leans into her husband's chest and he rests his chin on her head. "What a whirlwind, eh?"

Ansel exhales a long stream of air through his nostrils. "I'll say."

He's spent the past hour disassembling the backyard. All the chairs have been stacked and the tables folded. He'll have Kai help him load the truck later today and return the furniture to the rental agency at some point tomorrow.

"As much as I feel for everyone involved," Sophie says, "I have to admit that I'm glad it worked out this way. It's not that I dislike Max—I don't—but he's too..." Her voice trails away as she searches for a word. "Rigid?"

"Uncreative," Ansel substitutes.

"Unappreciative of creativity," Sophie decides.

"Unappreciative of *Piper's* creativity," Ansel says, and knows this has ultimately always been the problem.

JANE.

Saturday, 3:42p.m. (PDT)

Despite the dry heat, the cotton of Jane's tank top clings to her sticky back. She'd slathered SPF 30 up and down her arms before embarking on the hike, but she can still feel her shoulders beginning to burn. "Can we stop for a minute?" she asks Marcus, grabbing hold of his wrist and halting his stride. She stands behind him and unzips the backpack he wears, rummaging through its contents for sunscreen. "I need to reapply really quickly."

Up ahead, Kai points something out to her brothers, likely volunteering information pertaining to Bend. Wildlife, mountains, the history of the city... Whatever it is, Jane's sure he won't mind repeating the lesson once she and Marcus catch up.

"It's crazy to think that I should be getting ready to walk down the aisle with Max's best man right now, isn't it?" The wedding had been scheduled for four o'clock, with an abundance of dancing to follow. It occurs to her that she won't be critiquing the fancy footwork of Maxwell Terrence Storm, III, Esq., and that they will probably never attend a concert together. "At least the bridesmaids' dresses are decent. I might still be able to get some use out of mine."

Marcus snorts. "Trying to look on the bright side, I see."

Jane smears a bit of the coconut-scented lotion on her shoulders before returning it to the bag. Then she spins her boyfriend to face her and leans up to plant a kiss on his lips. "For the record," she says, "I know you're the one."

"You do, huh? What makes you so sure?"

"A number of things, really. You make me laugh and you pay attention to even the most mundane details of my stories. You're also handsome and smart and incredibly kind. Plus, you don't mind the fact that I have smelly feet or that I often have a patch of overly long hair on my knee because I seem to miss that same spot every time I shave. Oh! And you're a really good kisser." Jane kisses him a second time to reinforce this statement, allowing her lips to linger on his. "If you were to ask me to marry you, I would definitely say yes."

Marcus smiles and slips his hand into hers, the embrace slick and warm thanks to sunscreen and sweat. "That's excellent information to know for *when* I ask you, because at this point, there's no 'if' about it."

JONNY.

Saturday, 8:08p.m. (MDT)

With ninety minutes to kill at the Denver International Airport, Jonny loops his backpack over his shoulder and meanders through the terminal in search of someplace to grab a drink. He finds a spot not far from his next gate and sidles up to the bar.

"Will you be needing a food menu?" the bartender asks.

"Just a beer, thanks. I'll try whatever it is you've got on tap from Great Divide." A moment later, he sits with his lager and pulls out his phone. Ignoring the messages that had arrived while he was in the air, he scrolls through his contacts until the words "Piper Astoria Ferguson" are highlighted. Then he opens a new text box and writes, "So... I'm sitting at a bar in the Denver airport and it just occurred to me that I never made it to that Mexican restaurant you told me to check out if I was ever in Radio Park. Olé, right? Great guac and sea bass tacos?" His thumb hovers over the keypad for only a few seconds before sending the correspondence.

He doesn't suggest a return trip; he's hoping he won't need to be the one to do that.

A moment later, his phone vibrates and he glances at the screen. "Maybe you'll have to come back for another visit," Piper has written.

Right after this, a follow-up text appears: "Or I can come to you! I've never tried surfing before and think it would be fun."

Jonny grins and relaxes into his seat, his thumbs composing an answer. "I'd like that," he responds. "I'd like that a lot." And then, summoning a few extra ounces of courage and honesty, he adds, "I'm really glad we found the way back to one another, Piper."

THE WAY BACK
Playlist

"By and By" – Caamp

"Strange American Dream" – Rayland Baxter

"Going, Going, Oregon" – The Fat Handsome

"(If You're Wondering If I Want You To) I Want You To" – Weezer

"First in Flight" – Don McCloskey

"The Bagend March" – Bella's Bartok

"Alone" – Trampled By Turtles

"Where We Are" – The Lumineers

"Twisted Fate" – The Suitcase Junket

"Farmhouse" – Phish

"8 Dogs 8 Banjos" – Old Crow Medicine Show

"Way Back" – Reel Big Fish

"Just Wonderin'" – Caamp

Acknowledgments

The person I'd most like to thank here is someone who wants zero recognition. However, just know that I went to college with an incredibly talented musician who had the most amazing curls and this voice that contained *so much emotion* every time he sang. I don't know how to put into words how his voice used to make me feel. I think the highest compliment I can offer is that listening to him made me want to write.

Anyway, he was in a band that I adored (they once told me I was an honorary band member because I attended so many shows, and whether *they* remember saying that or not, *I'll* never forget it!) and later went on to produce a solo album. There was a song on that solo album that should actually come before Caamp's "By and By" on the playlist preceding these acknowledgments, but I didn't list it because he doesn't want to be credited. So... that's the guy who really deserves to be recognized. You know who you are, and thank you.

But there are some others who should be recognized as well! My mom, Nancy Newman, and my other mother, Amy Gorman, are deserving of many, many accolades. The two of them read everything I write... first drafts, second drafts... even thirtieth drafts if I were to ask them to!

Regarding the promotion of this novella, Mary McDannell has been a wealth of information when it comes to #booktoks and Jody Dickey actually helped me make one! (She flew the airplane while I filmed.)

I think it goes without saying that every single person who reads my blog and encourages me to keep pursuing this nearly impossible mission to obtain a literary agent should receive at least a dozen pats on the back.

Probably more. Special shoutout to my Pat-and-Patti Fan Club because those ladies shower me with praise from the west coast to the east!

Here's a funny little side story: When my mom was reading this for the first time, she said something along the lines of, "I knew it was going to have a happy ending, but I couldn't wait to get to it!" In actuality, the original version of this novella had a very *unhappy* ending: Jonny never met up with Piper and stayed in an unsatisfying relationship with Alex instead, Piper *did* marry Max, and Jane broke up with Marcus because she didn't believe he was the one. I fixed it this time around. Sometimes, a happy ever after is needed in life, you know?

Back to the acknowledgements...

I am so appreciative of EVERYONE who is willing to read about the many, many characters who reside in my head. I only hope that you someday *really* get to meet Sebastian. He is, and always will be, my absolute favorite.

12727140R00142